CHARLES ANTHONY JACKSON

ISBN: 978-1-961017-64-1 (sc)
ISBN: 978-1-961017-65-8 (e)

Rev. date: 07/09/2023

CONTENTS

CHAPTER 1

Awakening

IT WAS A NORMAL DAY in the neighborhood. Nobody expected the day to be any different than usual. Therefore, there were children parading themselves outside and making loud noises outside Tobias' window during the morning time. Although, the neighborhood wasn't the safest, but all was quiet inside Tobias' home. Then a loud thunder sound of a rainstorm occurred and the children took off running for overhead cover. He wasn't a bit surprised because it was Friday, a regular school day in October. A few middle school children would pause by Tobias outside bedroom window, then continue passing, before going to school because the bus stop was so close to his house.

Tobias' mother inside the home, prepared herself for the ungrateful message, she had to tell Tobias. She would be informing Tobias; they would be going to visit her friend Dundry. Tobias mother's name who was Ms. Elle, loved to visit people. Ms. Elle believed visiting people was the neighborly thing to do, if you wanted to have friends. Once a week, she would make a duty to visit an acquaintance and establish a friendship with somebody. Sometimes, Ms. Elle would have her son Tobias with her and sometimes she wouldn't. A lot of times, Tobias would be left with his father, while he wondered if his mother was safe. Either way, Ms. Elle dreaded to have this talk with Tobias.

Tobias who was a middle-age child, would always pray nothing would happen bad to his mother or too anyone. He wished his father would deny, his mother the right to go visit acquaintances every week. Tobias would hear from others about the neighborhood not being safe. From his own personal experiences, Tobias knew the neighborhood was not safe. Albeit, he dared not explain his feelings to no one. The feelings, which lay deep inside Tobias, were too great. It was tortures for Tobias, when he heard someone becoming a victim of sexual abuse, harassment or rape. It was also a despair, for Tobias to try and explain to his father about his aspirations.

Therefore, Tobias kept his feelings to himself, but sometimes his feelings became so strong, he had to show concern. This was why, Tobias decided to travel with his mother over to her friend's house. Dundry the mother's friend, was a tall slender woman with jet black hair, black eyes, and an almond brown complexion. It appeared to Tobias, Ms. Dundry was in her late thirties or early forties. Ms. Dundry talked with a soothing voice. She was kind and dressed pleasantly. During Tobias initial greeting with Ms. Dundry, instantly his mother and he felt at home inside her place. The smell of sweet smelling incents went all through the home.

Then, Ms. Dundry shouted, "Melvin come from back there in your bedroom. I want you to meet someone!" Melvin rushed to his mother's eager requested call. Tobias glanced and paused. Then, he realized this was no ordinary person. It was a student from his school, who he vaguely recognized. Every time he saw the student, a state of confusion occurred. Melvin seemed to be nice, but something was different about him. Something he couldn't analyze. Something he just couldn't understand. It was an intimidation, which he never experienced. An intimidation, which did not come from someone who was bigger or stronger; but an intimidation, which came from not understanding. Melvin showed, wearing a tight white tee shirt and light tight blue jean shorts, which the crotch went up his bottom cheeks. Tobias instantly drew closer to his mother Ms. Elle.

Ms. Dundry announced to Tobias for him not to be shy from her son. She informed, her son Melvin only dresses differently because he believed, woman attire was pretty and fun to wear. Tobias tried to be understanding and friendly. He looked passed his phobia and concerns. The thought of only one neighborly visit, stayed in his mind. So, Tobias tried to be friendly to Melvin because of his mother and Ms. Dundry. Although, deep down inside, emotions build inside him. Nobody knew of Tobias' past experiences. Tobias stayed on high alert during the entire situation because he was young, but not so naïve. Melvin informed him; he would direct him to his toys and grabbed his hand.

Tobias realized he was big for his age, early in life. His mother had trouble finding clothes in the children's section, which would fit him. Tobias would have to wear adult clothes as a child. Nevertheless, his mind was still childlike. Perhaps, because of Tobias' size, he was mistaken for being competent of his decisions. Tobias became a sex victim. No one knew, except for few members who participated with his football team. This made him conscience of his activities. Therefore, Tobias had an objective, to prevent unwanted, unexpected or undesired sexual behavior. He chose to protect himself and anyone else who desired to be free from sex offenders. Tobias hoped he could make a difference in life and help somebody.

When Melvin grabbed Tobias' hand, he skipped along as if he thought the two of them were a couple made in heaven. Once Tobias reached Melvin's bedroom, he jerked his hand away from Melvin's hand. Initially, Tobias began to scold Melvin about holding his hand. Tobias notified Melvin; he did not believe in holding another boy's hand. Melvin sarcastically told Tobias for him not to be offended. This was his way of becoming friends with someone new. Melvin opened his toy box; and Tobias became excited. Inside the toy box were a variety of toys, which any middle-age boy would enjoy having. When Tobias began to savior with all the different toys, Melvin stood back and just observed.

Inside the toy box was an exclusive limit edition racetrack. Tobias only dreamed of playing with such a racetrack. He took all the assorted pieces out and put the track together. The track was brand new, and straight out the package. As Tobias began assembling the track, Melvin informed him; he was happy because Tobias was having a good time. Although, by observation, Melvin was not playing and not having fun. Eventually, Tobias question Melvin. Tobias wanted to know, why Melvin was not playing with his toys. Melvin informed to Tobias; he had a secret, which his mom hated. Also, he informed Tobias; he didn't play with his toys in the toy box. His real toys were in the closet.

Melvin showed Tobias, his personal stash of toys, he had hidden in the closet. It was an assortment of women's clothes and wigs. Tobias promised he would not notify anyone about the women's clothes and how Melvin liked to cross dress. He instructed Melvin; peradventure, if he had the urge to wear women's clothing, he should only do it in the presence of his bedroom. This is because his mother informed him of this. Furthermore, Melvin inquired from Tobias, would he make a pretty girl when he was dressed like a woman. Tobias notified he was an ugly display of a pretty girl. Then, Melvin appeared sad. So, Tobias informed Melvin; although, if dressing like a girl made him happy, then he should be happy.

Surprisingly, Melvin became so relieved of Tobias approval. Melvin's first response was to kiss Tobias on the mouth. He tried to kiss Tobias. Unfortunately, Tobias took it ungratefully. Melvin informed Tobias; he thought Tobias was handsome and kind. Sadly, he wanted Tobias to like him. Melvin informed Tobias; he wanted to start a romantic relationship with Tobias. Tobias realized he was in a situation, which he didn't anticipate. Although, he did want to be friends with Melvin. Even though, at first sight, Tobias did not want to be friendly. Fortunately, now, it became clear. Melvin was not so strange after all. He was different than himself most definitely, but not totally strange. Tobias knew Melvin was lonely because he did not think, he had friends in school.

Tobias informed Melvin; they could only be friends. He had sympathy for Melvin and his feelings. Tobias recognized while they were playing together and Melvin was dressed up in his women's attire, Melvin appeared to be free with happiness. Tobias never noticed Melvin being happy in school. Melvin carry himself sad and lonely during school hours because he had no friends. Tobias figured he would be Melvin's friend in school, but not have a romantic relationship. Tobias informed Melvin; he only looked at girls romantically. Melvin appeared to comprehend Tobias message; and Tobias met Melvin the next day at school.

Tobias returned the next day at school. He noticed Melvin was upbeat as he greeted him hello. Then, during class recess, Tobias notice guys making trouble with Melvin. Melvin shouted out to Tobias, to attract his attention. Decidedly, Tobias figured to investigate because Melvin and he were friends now. Sadly, the guys who were making trouble with Melvin, began questioning Tobias's relationship with Melvin. Melvin voluntarily answered and informed them, he's my friend. The guys started laughing and informed him; he was lucky he had a bodyguard because they were going to kick his booty. Melvin thanked Tobias for his assistance and offered to do him any kind of favor. Tobias informed Melvin; he wasn't a bodyguard but a booty guard because them guys were going to kick his booty.

Unknowingly by Tobias, other unpopular school kids observed the event which happened to Melvin. They never seen a student stand up and protect a gay person. It was remarkable to them and they wanted help with their situation. The school students asked, "Was this something, which he felt strongly about?" They wanted to know was he gay or maybe he had a vendetta. Tobias only informed because of his beliefs; he believed no one should feel bullied because of sex, orientation or circumstances. Surprisingly, school children would ask him, if a sex crime was occurring in his presence, would he help to prevent the crime and would he be their protector. Tobias informed, if they would do their part to prevent sex crimes, then he would do his share to be a duty guard. They called him the Booty Guard.

One individual day on a Saturday morning, a couple of Tobias' friends decided to come together and play a friendly game of football. Tobias had one known associate from his Little League Football Team, who would come and visit him. His friend was named Ricky. Tobias' friend named Ricky would converse to him about all the pretty girls, he met during the day. Most of the girls attended Tobias school because Ricky and Tobias both attended the same school. It appeared to Tobias; Ricky was going through a puberty crisis because he would complain about not having a girlfriend. To Tobias, it all seemed so silly, since they were only in the eighth grade. Although, Ricky took the situation real serious.

As everyone of Tobias' associates gathered outside on the playing field to participate in sandlot football, there were outside spectators gathered around also. (For whomever, who do not know what the definition of sandlot football was; the definition term is backyard football played primary by young people. Additionally, it was played with less equipment and rules than sanction football). Although, Tobias playing field was about a half mile away from his home, which he enjoyed the walk because this gave him the time to warm-up before playing. Before the football game began, Tobias observed in the spectator crowd, pretty girls sitting on the ground. Instantly, Ricky's attention became focus on the pretty girls.

Tobias figured it was going to be a problem with Ricky, the guys and these pretty schoolgirls watching the sandlot football game. The reasons why; when young schoolboys from the ghetto are not supervised properly, things could go bad. Even though, during the beginning of the football game, deciding which players were going to be on which team, was a chore. Then, when it came to Ricky's choice of teams, he kept talking about the pretty girls sitting on the sidelines of the field. Tobias got fed up with all the distractions of the pretty girls, but he tried to keep it to himself. Furthermore, he enjoyed looking at pretty girls too, but he did not want it to be a distraction from the game.

It became a point, where Tobias finally told Ricky. Tobias informed Ricky; if he wanted to communicate with the girls on the sideline, then he had to exit out the football game. In addition, Ricky began talking rude to the schoolgirls. At one point, Ricky told a schoolgirl, she was a tramp and no good slut. Sadly, this schoolgirl was a respected student in the school. Tobias observed the incident and became conscience of the problem. He believed the situation was becoming out of hand and somebody had to put a stop to the craziness. Tobias informed Ricky; leave the girls along because they do not want him. Then, Ricky tried to embarrass Tobias by calling him gay because he respected people's rights to peace from sexual harassment.

For some unknown reason, Ricky never really forgave Tobias, for correcting his behavior in public. Ricky believed Tobias thought he was better than he. He wondered was Tobias being genuine to others or was he putting on a front. Maybe, Tobias was gay because he never seen him talking to any girls. Ricky made a deal with himself; he was going to get even with Tobias for embarrassing him in front of friends. After a Little League Football game which Tobias played, Ricky played a cruel trick on Tobias. Ricky informed Tobias and other football players, there was a pretty schoolgirl who cheerlead with his football team, who has a romantic affection for Tobias. She wanted to meet Tobias under the bleachers.

Tobias became so excited. He wanted to know, who this pretty cheerleader was because he was excited about meeting people too. The cheerleader stood under the bleachers in the shade. Tobias couldn't get a good look at her, while she was in the shade. The cheerleader kept suggesting for Tobias to come closer because she loved him and wanted a romantic relationship with him. There were other football players listening also. Tobias came closer to the cheerleader. He was so excited; he could barely keep his composer. As Tobias came closer, football players on his team began to laugh. The idea of something being this funny, made Tobias wonder, what was happening.

Tobias approached the cheerleader. The cheerleader had her back facing towards him. The person kept repeating, "I love you; and I am so crazy about you". Tobias walked right next to her and touched her on her back. In Tobias' mind, he kept thinking, she looked so familiar. Although, she was different in a way. The cheerleader turned around and said, "I love you". It was Melvin! Tobias became angry with Melvin. Melvin notified Tobias; Ricky told me, you are shy and you love me. Tobias explained to Melvin; you and I are just friends. There is no love affair between us and will never be. Melvin, you should know this by now! Melvin became disappointed and sad.

Unfortunately, it appeared Melvin still did not fully comprehend the friendship between Tobias and him. Luckily, Tobias did not take it too personal. He continued giving his booty guard service to Melvin because he needed it. Melvin was always into trouble with some prejudice redneck or prejudice ghetto thug, who did not understand the heart of Melvin. Tobias had sympathy for Melvin, but he was not gay because he loved women. He loved women so much; he thought about them every day. Tobias would have these fantasies; he would meet the most beautiful woman in the world. Then, he would wake up in a cold sweat from his shorts to his underwear.

There was a girl football cheerleader, who noticed Tobias the Booty Guard as being interesting. She was an associate of Melvin's and inquired about more the services of the Booty Guard. Even though, Melvin was worried about the girl's interest, Melvin informed the cheerleader of Tobias whereabouts. The football cheerleader was named Sherri; and she was beautiful. She stood about 5 foot, 6 inches, had above average smart and a cheerleader's built. When Sherri walked, everyone noticed, she walked with a purpose. School teachers recognized Sherrie for charism and motivational skills. Unfortunately, sometimes being beautiful came with a curse.

Sherri wanted protection from the overbearing football players, who prayed on innocent cheerleaders. Whenever available, the football players would make inhumane suggestions. Sherri considered herself as a role model. There was nothing more exciting to her, then her abilities to be respected and cheer for her school football team. Sherri was not going to allow anyone in her power to intimidate her. Although, the intimidation at times, started to become a problem. So, when Melvin talked about his boyfriend being a Booty Guard, she became curious. She wanted the chance to find out, how she could be protected by Tobias, the Booty Guard. Tobias and Sherri acquaintance became awkward because Sherri's beauty made Tobias nervous and he appeared shy.

Even-though, Tobias appeared to be nervous and shy, his physique was over shadowing. Tobias had the size of a Senior High School student, but he was only in the eighth grade. There were few students at his age, who were bigger or stronger. Some say, "Tobias could rip a soda can in two parts with his bare hands". Then, his hand motions were quick as a fly. The State of North Carolina listed Tobias as the most athletic football player in his age bracket and predicted, he would break all the High School records in the book, if he participated in sports for High School. To add extra, Tobias was even a smart kid. Nevertheless, Tobias didn't like violence, unless it was necessary; and you almost had to make him mad, for him to use physical force against you.

With this information being given, Tobias enjoyed being anybody's booty guard in school. Tobias did not protect students because of any reason. If a student got in a fight for reasons of theft, anger or anything else besides of a sexual assault, then this was for some other kind of security guard. Tobias main concern was strictly sexual assault. He did not like sexual misconduct given. It was because the events in his past, which happened to him, and the individuals who had been sexually violated. This was a sickening, evil and demeaning action, which Tobias could not allow to take place. Therefore, Tobias rushed to help Sherri in her time of need.

The job started out simple for Tobias. There weren't any students in their school, while Tobias walked with Sherri, who would make any sexual obscene gestures toward Sherri. If anybody started to ask Tobias about Sherri's and his relationship together, then he would say, "She is my sister or cousin". As time passed, Sherri began informing other students; Tobias was her boyfriend. Tobias didn't realize, Sherri was notifying students; they were having a romantic relationship. If he had known, this was going to happen, he would have not committed to becoming Sherri's Booty Guard. It was too late for him to stop. Now, he felt obligated to block any student from making the slightest sexual advance to Sherri.

Tobias became more than a Booty Guard. He was her weapon of mass destruction for any unwanted advances from students. Sherri believed every kid who looked at her the wrong way, Tobias was supposed to make a big deal about it. Sherri was not his girlfriend, but he wished she was, since he was her Booty Guard. Finally, Tobias got fed up with running all the guys away, who might even try to think perverted of Sherri. No student boy would even try to mingle with Sherri now, except Melvin. Although, deep down inside, Tobias had thoughts for Sherri. He wanted passionately to touch her, kiss her, and do all kinds of freaky things to her. Tobias couldn't get it out of his head. Which is why, he had to stop giving her the booty duty.

Tobias figured to relieved him of his desires, he would ask Sherri for a date. Therefore, he walked up to Sherri and asked, "Could he meet her at a restaurant?" Sherri was confused. She figured; maybe, the job had become too dangerous for him. Tobias informed; something has made him become different towards her needs and the problem of her wanting not to be harassed by guys, who prey on girls for sexual needs. Tobias notified; he can control them guys, but he cannot control himself. He asked, "Could he kiss her and hold her in his arms?" Sherri refused. She told him, "He had befriended her, only to be able to make sexual advances for himself". This caused Tobias shame and sadness. Tobias decided to take a break from being the Booty Guard.

Nevertheless, Tobias' football season with the Little League Football Team ended. Finally, Sherri got a break from cheerleading from the Jr. High School football off season games; and Tobias had little contact with Sherri. Tobias assumed; Sherri occurred less of a problem, now with football players. Word passed around; Tobias no longer gave booty duty protection. Tobias mainly prepared himself for the 9th grade in High School. His mother Elle began keeping Tobias' cousin named Mercedes.

This took Tobias a while to get adjusted too. Although, Tobias enjoyed Mercedes company. Tobias made it a duty, to inform Mercedes to be safe when traveling from home, while back and forth to school in the neighborhood. Albeit, he knew, the neighborhoods were not safe.

When Mercedes arrived at school, she tried to be on her best behavior because she was at a different school. The only reason, why Mercedes decided to change schools because she didn't feel welcomed at her old school. At Mercedes' old school, she felt the boys were immature; and she had no friends. Furthermore, Mercedes had no siblings to associate with at home. Mercedes was an extravert individual and hated not to be able to refer with somebody her age, when she wanted too. Her parents believed; she was being difficult to live with in their house because Mercedes was spoiled rotten. Mercedes had access to everything she needed, except a lot of family and friends to support her social needs.

Tobias and Mercedes blended along good. Mercedes was like a little sister to Tobias; but she really, was his cousin. They were similar in age, and Tobias only felt compassion to be his cousin's Booty Guard, when needed. He even informed Mercedes; she didn't have to worry about any student boys sexually harassing her or trying to make sexual advances to her. Tobias made it known; he was her Booty Guard for life. Although, Mercedes made it clear; she didn't expect any boys to make sexual propositions at her. Even-though, Mercedes notified she did want to acquire friends, who had good moral judgement. The most important mission for Mercedes, was for herself to receive a good educational experience at her new school and establish good relationships with family and acquaintances.

Mercedes, who was escorted by her cousin Tobias on her first day, was happy to meet different acquaintances. She met certain students, who praised her for being a cousin of Tobias. Then, Mercedes met Melvin, who welcomed her acquaintance. Next, Melvin introduce Mercedes to Sherri, and immediately informed her; Sherri was Tobias' girlfriend fantasy. Sherri notified she was nobody's girlfriend fantasy. Her fantasy was making good grades in school and cheerleading. Ricky walked by and introduced himself as the High School football captain of the High School Football Team. Melvin informed them the football captain was the designated picker for the cheerleading queen. Sherri eyes opened wide and informed to Ricky; she would be the perfect cheerleading queen.

Ricky informed to Sherri; they must meet privately, for them to discuss the details of cheerleading queen. Meanwhile, Mercedes and Melvin talked about the benefits of having Tobias around them. It appeared; Tobias was becoming well popular in school. Although, rumors were spreading, how Tobias made sexually unwanted advances at Sherri. Mercedes didn't like the rumors and Melvin acknowledged; he didn't like the comments either. Therefore, Mercedes informed Tobias; he must be careful, for whom he performed booty duty to. Tobias could not believe; word had gotten out he made a sexual advance at Sherri. It was his own fault. Sherri's beauty made Tobias weak at times. Tobias realized he must be stronger, if he truly wants to be a servant for sexually abused victims.

Days later, before the end of the school year and summer break began, Tobias' parents work schedules had picked up heavy. Sadly, there wasn't a parent available, who could check on Mercedes for her cheerleading audition. Therefore, Tobias felt, for it to be especially important for him to be on his best booty guard duty for his cousin. Word got out at the school, Mercedes had been influenced by Melvin, for her to be a school cheerleader. Tobias respected cheerleaders, but he knew, his job would be harder now. To prevent his cousin Mercedes from encountering unwanted sexual propositions, Tobias rushed to the school to monitor Mercedes audition for the school cheerleading squad. An awakening had occurred to Tobias. Booty guard duty was not exclusive.

As Tobias arrived on the football field, he seen no people on the football field auditioning for a cheerleader. What he did see, was a handful of off-season football players in plain clothes walking around the football coaches' box office, which looked over the football stadium. Tobias inquired to a student; where are the cheerleaders? The student reported they are with the football players in the coaches' box office. Tobias, who was well over 6-foot-tall, looked through a window at the top of the door. He witnessed two students were blocking the door entrance from opening on the inside. It appeared Sherri and Mercedes were held hostage. Tobias with all his strength, pushed the coaches' box office door open. The two guys, who were blocking the door fell over.

Ricky announced; hey, you are not the only Booty Guard around here. Tobias walked over to him and announced, "What you say?" This was the only comment, before Tobias hit him square in the nose. Tobias spotted Sherri pulling her underwear up under her cheerleading skirt. He became extremely angry and began punching four guys in the area. Mercedes was crying for help because blood was coming from everywhere. Next, the girls ran out the area quickly, through the door. Tobias was thrown out the door by the four guys. Blood was coming out of Tobias mouth profusely. One guy informed Tobias to go home; and don't come back in here. Ricky announced we are the only Booty Guards around here; and I will kill you, if I get my hands on you.

Tobias looked at his cousin Mercedes. Then, he looked at Sherri and became sick to his stomach. The thought about Sherri having sex with Ricky; it made him vomit. Tobias realized he still had strong feelings, which was emotional for Mercedes. He was laying on the ground and sat up. Although, Tobias crave the feeling of reentering the coaches' box office to fight Ricky again. He was too sick. Mercedes kept repeating to Sherri, "You are okay? We can make a call to the Police, if you have been raped". Sherri acknowledge, she was okay; and it wasn't all so bad. Tobias was confused and bewildered. He felt guilty. Tobias figured he was supposed to be Sherri's Booty Guard; and he had abandoned her. Sherri had become a victim by Ricky. This only made Tobias angry and feeling worst off. Tragically, Tobias believed he still had a romantic effect for Sheri.

Days passed; Tobias started High School. The High School called North City Town where Tobias attended, consumed basically the same students as his Jr. High School. Although, North City Town was bigger and taught more students from grades 9th through 12th. Tobias first day in High School was a little intimidating, but he believed; friends from his old school would make it more welcoming. Besides, his cousin Mercedes arrived too school with him. Also, Melvin was already there on the first day of school and spreading talk about Tobias. Then, Tobias observed Sherri in the school cafeteria. Unfortunately, Sherri was still socializing with Ricky.

Surprisingly, they were calling themselves an item. Tobias could not believe; Sherri would stoop so low as to call Ricky her boyfriend.

Some guy, who was inside the coaches' box office during Sherri's rape, made eye contact with Mercedes. The guy made a glaring look at Mercedes. Then, the guy whispered something provocative to Mercedes. Tobias could tell Mercedes became offended because Mercedes drew away defensively. Tobias walked up to the guy. The guy stood up erect as in a defensive position. Tobias mentioned, if he sees one more time, another football player who is trying to solicit his cousin. Tobias promised, he was going to punch somebody's nose off. All the ex-Jr. High School football players, which was a good handful, stood up in defiance. Tobias screamed, for them to come on, if they want to test their fighting skills.

It was no use; this guy was relentless for Mercedes. Tobias caught this guy staring at Mercedes and trying to contact Mercedes without her approval. Mercedes fell in despair. Helplessly, she confided with Tobias, about the guy bothering her. Therefore, Tobias met up with the guy personally. This guy was name Persia and bragged about his strength. Also, he bragged about his athletic abilities. The guy would wear weightlifting shirts, which showed the amount of weight he could lift. He was approximately 6 feet tall and had very large biceps. Although, Tobias was not intimidated or impressed. He wanted to fight this guy because the guy was a nuisance to his cousin and him. Tobias made plans to meet the guy on the street for battle.

When Persia met Tobias on the street, he walked with companions. Persia was one of four students totaled, walking towards Tobias. Tobias immediately, spoke on his behalf to the other three students. He knew he was outnumbered and at an unfair disadvantage. To reason with the other students, Tobias informed the three students; you all can leave because you all are not a part of this mess. The three students stayed stationary, observing Tobias. Ricky was a part of the three students also. Tobias began shouting extremely loud. He informed he was warning the others because they don't want this pain. No one decided to leave the area. Therefore, Tobias bald up his fist and began to run towards them.

Suddenly, a squeaky noise from a door slam was heard. Tobias and the other students stopped moving. A student girl came outside of her house to watch what was happening. The student girl, who was attractive and attended High School said, "What you all are getting ready to do". Ricky informed to the student girl; they were going to smash some head. The little girl asked, "Who's head?" Persia became angry with the girl. Persia informed the girl; she needed to return inside her house and allow people to handle their business. The student girl attended North City Town High School also. Her name was Tammy; and she was feisty. Tammy recognized the guys as her High School students. Then, she recognized Tobias from descriptions by other students.

Tammy informed she knew who Tobias was because he was the Booty Guard. She greeted Tobias with hello. Tobias informed, hello to her also. Tammy instantly notified Melvin by phone; his friend Tobias was about to fight some High School students. Next, she distracted the students from fighting by asking Tobias, did he have super strength and could he rip a soda can in two with his bare hands. Tobias informed he had done it before and probably, could do it again. Tammy found him a vegetable can. Tobias took the can and squeezed. The can busted with an explosion. Then, Tobias ripped the can in two with his bare hands. Ricky informed Persia; go ahead and punch Tobias in the nose. Persia flexed his biceps and backed away.

Footsteps were heard by the High School students coming closer. The students turned around to see, what direction the footsteps were coming from. It was coming quickly behind them. Mercedes and Melvin were running up close with sticks in their hands. Ricky informed to his friends; don't be afraid because they still outnumbered them. Then, Tammy came out in the street and stood beside Melvin and Mercedes. Next, Tobias looked at the group of student guys and took a two by four stick and broke it into pieces. The group of student High School guys began running away, one by one, until no one was left. Tobias was surprised he scared them away, but he was relieved. He politely, thanked Tammy and the rest of his associates for all their help.

Therefore, Tobias considered Tammy needed the booty guard service as well. Tammy became a little different than his regular booty guard client. She would notify Tobias; she was in stress, only to find her safe. Then, Tammy would feel on his muscles or rub his face. Sometimes, Tammy would suggest perverted things or do perverted things to him. Tammy called him a tease, but Tobias tried to keep his clients and him in a plutonic relationship. It appeared she wanted Tobias sexually. Sexual relations confused Tobias because he did not know where the line ended from wanted and unwanted sex with someone. During one instance, Tammy called him on a distress call to her home; and she was alone. When Tobias arrived, she hugged him and gave him a passionate kiss.

Tammy informed she wanted Tobias to be her boyfriend. Even-though, Tobias felt strongly for them to stay friends. Feelings got involved between them quickly. Soon, Tammy told Tobias, to break her virginity. Although, Tobias was a virgin also. However, Tobias thought, maybe, this was a sign for him to have a girlfriend. So, Tammy and Tobias got extremely cozy. They laid together romantically half the night. Although, they were both inexperience with sex. As they became sexually interment, sickness occurred to Tobias. Tobias had a secret conscientious objective to performing certain sex acts. Tammy became upset and figured; Tobias was turned off with having a sexual relationship with her. Tobias knew he had acquired a sex phobia; so, they settled on being friends

North City Town High School was a school with promiscuous young students. School crimes consisting of sexual harassment, rape and sexual abuse happened on a frequent bases without any recognition from most students and staff. In most cases, there were little or nonexistent upgrades for student's safety in North City Town High School. The school resided on 10 acres of lush green grass and Prime real estate inside the city of Winston-Salem, NC. The school looked like a place which could be owned by a College Campus or government corporation. Furthermore, the facility was maintained well. Which, it was scandalous because the neighbors who lived in the neighborhoods around the school, were sometimes corruptive, vindictive, and ruthless people.

Tobias as a young baby boy grew up in a respected home. His mother Elle was a hardworking woman, who establish herself as a high paid manager for an apparel company. Also, Tobias' daddy named Rogers, was a plane engine mechanic for an International Airline Company. There was one sibling to Tobias, a stepbrother named Reggie. Although, Reggie resided in the state of Texas. Therefore, Tobias considered himself a single child, who grew up with the hard knocks of learning the do's and don'ts of life. Despite the rough learning, he was happy with the amount of knowledge, he had acquired. In recognition of his age, Tobias was still a youngster. Tobias knew, he had a lot more to learn in his life. After High School, he expected to further his education at some well-known institution.

It was a blessing for Tobias, to be loved by family and associates. Tobias believed it was no mistake of his good fortunes because he trusted in God. His family ritual was to read the bible, pray every night and attend church on Sundays. This is the reason, Tobias figured he allowed a sexual assault to occur on his guard. At one point in his life, there wasn't enough thought of God. A lack of righteousness and perseverance, which Tobias took for granted was his own weakness. Adults took it for granted, Tobias had the capacity to do whatever he wanted to do, if he chose to do it. No power except God's power could change this. Mindfully, Tobias trained himself to think the same. Fortunately, Tobias knew he would get distracted occasionally and only the power of God would help.

Reggie, who was Tobias stepbrother, was concerned. He loved Tobias and wanted the best for him. Even-though, Rogers the father, was a bit naïve. If Tobias had any problems, then Tobias would confide with Reggie. Peradventure, Reggie decided to visit Tobias because he was the older sibling. Therefore, Reggie thought he could correct Tobias flaws. Tobias informed to Reggie about his fear of sexual relationships. The thought of any abnormal behavior by Tobias, and Reggie reacted extremely worried. It was nothing too difficult for Reggie, if he had to fix Tobias sex phobia. Nevertheless, when he arrived in the town of Winston-Salem, NC, he put on his gigolo clothes (attire bought to impress women) and venture out on the streets in Tobias' neighborhood.

Rumors in the neighborhood and at Tobias High School were notified to Reggie. Tobias spent a lot of time and energy becoming the Booty Guard and no appreciation was given by clients. Since Reggie was at least four years older than Tobias, he felt obligated to informed Tobias, his service was not wanted. Reggie explained, what women really wanted were sexual encounters and not for him to be a booty blocker or booty stopper. The example Reggie showed, were women walking and even prancing down the street in explicit tight clothing to show off their body. Convincing evidence were the failures of Tobias, which women were being protected from sexual predators and ended up having sexual encounters with their predators. Sadly, Tobias gave in to a sexual encounter himself by sexual persuasion.

Nevertheless, Tobias continued with his booty duty service because there was always somebody in distress. Tammy for instance, claimed unwanted boys would prey on her because she was alone mostly in her home. Her single parent mother worked a lot. So, Tammy's mother became comfortable with Tobias hanging around, giving Tammy the booty service. Melvin continue to be antagonized by conservative rights students and needed Tobias service. Further, Tobias' cousin Mercedes would always keep the booty guard service because she was his cousin. Then, other school students depended on Tobias' booty guard service as well. Tobias figured his school needed a service as this because of the student response and of his bad experience in school.

Who cared about Reggie's theories of the booty guard service; Tobias enjoyed giving the booty service because he had a sex phobia? One night, Tobias imagined this fantasy. Tobias fantasized he was this great Detective, working for a Victims' Crisis Unit of the State of North Carolina. People were getting rape, which were both men and women. The only evidence, which was given, was something of unknown origins were sexually molesting people. Police personnel would go inside this building to investigate, believing they were going to solve sex crimes and end up becoming sexually molested themselves. The building had no see through windows and it was a public building. Ironically, the building had a sign which read, "Fun for the young and old".

The building laid smack in the middle of the business district of Winston Salem, NC. There were people walking with sometimes tourist from other locations looking for attractions to attend. At first sight of the building, most people would think it was a museum or library. Then, people would notice the details someone took of the neon lights showing at night. The neon lights were fixed to decorate the building. Also, the building got more attention than the other buildings around it. It was a sturdy and very large building. By history name, the building was called the Kimbro building. Inside the building, there were opened space lofts and down below was the conference area. To enter the conference area, you would have to meet an attendant. Then, you could enter the main area.

Tobias as the Detective had a history of being loyal and diligent to his assignment. North Carolina Police Patrol knew with the background Tobias kept; he would do anything to be on the case of sex tragedies of Kimbro bldg. It was no accident; no detective or police officer wanted to be assigned the case of the Kimbro bldg. The reasons were because most attendees had fun or became sexually molested. Therefore, they introduce a special assistant for Tobias. The assistant had to be trained, but their qualifications were rare. The assistant's name was Saundra; and she had special training in combat and surveillance. Saundra recently had been assigned to Victims' Unit. Tobias began training her to investigate the case.

Saundra was bigger than Tobias. She stood 2 inches taller than Tobias 6-foot 1 frame. Her persona was humble because she loved a good joke and to laugh. Although, Saundra was slow to catch the punch line of a joke. Saundra occasionally acted like a special need person. Tobias had to repeat and demonstrate easily handled instructions to Saundra. He felt pity for Saundra difficulties to grasp an easy task. Even-though, Saundra was skilled and talented than most Police officers. Unfortunately, because of Saundra's dangerous job description, she carried scars on her body and face. Saundra's appearance was not very pleasing to the eyes. She had never experienced a romantic relationship and had few friends or acquaintances which she enjoyed.

Knowing the history of Saundra, Tobias kept secret eyes on her. Tobias believed Saundra was vulnerable to solicits. Therefore, he watched her back, when they were on duty assignment together. Tobias figured Saundra deserves different types of friends. Saundra needed friends, who could show her excitement. Also, someone who wouldn't judge her characteristics. Tobias knew his thoughts of friendship were a little old fashion. Furthermore, he introduced Saundra to Melvin to boost her social life. Together, Saundra and Melvin became friends. Then, soon, Melvin became interested in Tobias and Saundra's case with the sex tragedies of the Kimbro bldg. Although, Tobias continued to watch Saundra's back because she commented of being lonely.

While on a routine visit, Melvin requested to be chaperoned by Tobias and Saundra to a night of fun at the Kimbro bldg. Inside the Kimbro bldg., it was exciting. There was an open bay area with 108 different activities for the young and old. The lighting inside the area was lit like a casino. Each activity was separated by a petition or roll away wall. The man hosting the venue, was a tall and slender man. He had his back facing them, while monitoring the area. Tobias touched the man on the shoulder. Surprisingly, he was Tobias classmate Ricky. Prior to the visit, Tobias tried to inform Melvin about the risk, which was happening inside the Kimbro bldg. Melvin reminded Tobias; he had protection. His protection was from the Booty Guard and the 6'3 feet Saundra.

Ricky greeted them with alarm and had an astonishing look. He looked shocked and amazed. It appeared; Ricky had almost a loss of words. Then, Ricky regained his composer. Regardless of all the events occurring, Ricky announced he must give them a private tour. Detective Tobias insisted for Ricky, not to do anything special for them. Although, Ricky informed it was no hardship. During the private tour, an introduction was introduced of each activity. The activities were fun and some were educational. There were food tasting events, art training, music and dancing which were performed inside the bldg. At the end, visual display games were showcased. With the display games, Ricky informed, the best games required a monetary fee, which operated on the top floor.

Melvin persisted on knowing more about the top floor. Saundra volunteered to pay for the top floor. Tobias made sure, his supervision and protection would follow along with Melvin and Saundra. On the top floor, in a big size room, a gigantic computerized contraption machine which resembled an interactive spaceship was running. Buttons, handles and knobs were sporadic inside the contraption. Also, inside were different tasks for your body parts like connecting wires, massage devices and an instructions' monitor displaying activities inside. Once Ricky introduced the contraption, his demeanor changed. Ricky tried to persuade all three to enter. Although, Melvin and Saundra entered alone. Tobias assumed a person should observe first before participating.

As Melvin and Saundra entered the contraption, the room turned dark. The only lights which was shining, were on the outside of the contraption. A heartbeat was heard on the machine. Ricky inserted a disc drive inside the contraption to start the games inside the machine. Tobias heard computer noises. Then, singing, laughing, crying and cheering. It sounded like a sex movie was showing inside the contraption. Finally, the contraption stopped. Then, thump, thump, thump, thump as a sound was heard of a heartbeat slowing down. Melvin and Saundra exited with grins. They both rushed to confront Ricky and thank him for a satisfying experience. Tobias was confused. He inquired, what had happened? Ricky informed; the computer reads your body language. Then, analyze your sexual needs and desires.

CHAPTER 2

Duty Calls

RICKY INFORMED IT WAS TOBIAS turn next. Tobias noticed red marks were located on Melvin and Saundra skin. Also, he smelled a hint of fumes coming from the contraption. As Tobias steps inside the front entrance, a noise occurs as screech. Suddenly, Tobias steps back a half inch away. Tobias noticed fumes were dispersing in the inside. He walked back to Saundra and informed, there were fumes being released inside the contraption. Saundra notified with laughter; it is some sort of chemical drug, which makes you happy. Then, Melvin informed with laughter; he didn't care because the contraption made him feel sexually good. Tobias tried to prevent Melvin and Saundra from entering a second time. Melvin and Saundra avoided Tobias' warning because Ricky encourage the second round.

Next, Melvin and Saundra entered the contraption again. Ricky added more disc files into the contraption. The contraption began overheating. Inside the contraption, Melvin and Saundra believed, they were having the most exciting sexual experience of their life. Computers were analyzing Melvin and Saundra sexual desires as they were identifying both of their pleasures. Unfortunately, Melvin's sexual desires got crossed with Saundra's sexual desires. Machine devices which supposedly massage, ended up being torturous. A certain device began hitting Melvin in his private area. Also, Saundra began experiencing mechanical hands spanking her buttocks. This was neither one of their wishes. They both begin to scream for assistance.

Furthermore, Ricky began advising Tobias; the contraption normally was a safe satisfying operational machine. The contraption was overheating. The reason why, the machine was overheating was simple. Two people who were sex starved and had never been fed, causes the machine to overheat because the demand and their desires had the machine react in a negative way. The machine was built for mild, light, sexual foreplay. An extreme acceleration of its normal capacities and the fight to keep up causes the machine to overheat. Tobias informed Ricky; don't discuss the reasons but do something to shut this machine down. Then, Tobias rushed quickly inside the contraption to save the booty's of Melvin and Saundra. It became another job for Tobias (the Booty Guard).

Tobias as the Booty Guard ran inside the contraption and fought hand and hand with the devices, which tried to block his entrance. Melvin who was completely naked from the waste up was bleeding from his private area and tied to a lounge chair. A vibrating device which was hanging from the ceiling was going up and down on Melvin's private parts. For unknown reasons, Melvin would not stop smashing buttons and switching knobs with his access hand because the other one was tied up. Poor Saundra was laughing and screaming. She was tied face down on some sort of platform. A pair of boxing gloves attached to a device was pounding her buttocks. Tobias figured, maybe it was a massage device.

Finally, Tobias was able to free Melvin from the ropes of his lounge chair. In the process, other sex devices were thrown at them. Eventually, they were able to defend themselves from other devices and save Saundra booty too. During the entire ordeal, porno was showing on some projector screen. Sadly, Tobias vomited from all the obscene displays. With the little bit of strength Tobias possessed, he escorted Melvin and Saundra out the room into the hallways. Tobias made an acclamation; Melvin and Saundra needed to recognize their flaws. They each have sexual fantasies which they should keep closed for good reasons. All thoughts are not good thoughts and should not be disclosed. As with good intentions, evil thoughts may exist also.

Reggie decided to visit Tobias' High School. He observed Tobias escorting pretty girls to their bus. For no reason, Reggie hated the idea of Tobias having a booty guard service. It was wasted energy to Reggie because he thought all High School girls were sexual beings, which wanted sex consciously or unconsciously. Therefore, if the High School girls were preyed on by other boys, then who cared. Reggie thought these girls enjoyed the attention. Regardless, if some girls were experiencing stress and abuse. Life in High School for some girls consisted of this. Reggie believed it was the way High School was supposed to operate; and there shouldn't be a need for booty guard service. What Reggie figured was Tobias caused the interrupting of the flow to students' High School experiences.

Being the Booty Guard was not all fun for Tobias. Sometimes, Tobias would receive a lot of backlash from his High School classmates. When Tobias was a Freshman in High School, a High School Senior questioned his booty guard motives. The Senior was a girl named Tracy. Tracy was from the apartment projects, which was a bad neighborhood. A pretty girl, at 5 feet and 4 inches, Tracy was voluptuous and flirty. Tracy judged Tobias as someone who was only trying to get publicity or recognition in High School. Also, it didn't look good as Tobias appeared like a football jock only on the prey to impress High School girls. Tracy challenged Tobias as her Booty Guard, during her last days in High School. Tobias accepted the job, only because he wanted to prove acceptance of their peers.

One day, Tracy requested Tobias to escort her on the bus during her trip home. Tobias was not familiar with the apartment projects, but he did hear about bad people living in Tracy's neighborhood. Tobias knew he had bad people living in his neighborhood too. Although, there were mostly good people in his neighborhood also. Albeit, in Tracy's neighborhood, everyone was supposed to be bad. Therefore, Tracy carried herself tough to show, she stayed where the bad people existed. Tracy's flaw was she was beautiful and misleading. Which is why, Tracy needed Tobias. Tracy had flirted with the wrong boy in her neighborhood, who went to her school. This boy was a High School football player and a thug. The boy's name was Craig. Craig had no respect for girls in his High School.

The first impression of Craig, Tobias knew he was going to be trouble. Anytime someone looked at themselves as being superior because of their gender was a problem for Tobias. Although, Tobias was taller and bigger than Craig. Furthermore, Craig was a little bully, who had popular friends. It didn't matter because Tobias was going to create big problems for Craig, if he messed with Tracy. Sadly, he spotted Craig holding a submission hold on Tracy. Craig was on the verge of breaking Tracy's wrist from a vicious hand grip. Therefore, Tobias had to get involved. With one arm, reaching around Craig's neck by his bicep, Tobias just squeezed Craig's neck in a choke hold. Tobias informed to Craig; he was about to become his little girlfriend because Craig was hurting Tracy.

Therefore, Tobias made it a priority to chaperone Tracy, this individual day. This day was on a Friday; so therefore, no school was held the next day. For Tobias, it wasn't for personal reasons. It was all professional because he had his reputation on watch as the Booty Guard. The bus trip went smoothly for Tobias. Tracy and Tobias talked smoothly amongst each other. She was from the apartment projects; but she talked proper and intelligently. Tracy asked Tobias, "Had he ever ventured in her neighborhood before?" Tobias tried to sound confident. He informed he might have ventured through her neighborhood before, maybe once or twice. Truthfully, Tobias knew nothing about Tracy's neighborhood. Every bus turn made in Tracy's neighborhood, made Tobias nervous.

Once the school bus reached Tracy's residence, a clearly shaken Tobias exited the bus. Tracy tried to comfort Tobias by given him a handwritten direction's map of how to leave the apartment projects. It made Tobias a little more at ease; but clearly, he was still worried. As Tobias walked behind Tracy, he made sure to make 360 peripheral turns to gain a mental picture of easily identifiable surroundings. Tracy could tell he was worried and smiled at him. Tobias gave a return smile and followed quickly to Tracy's front porch. Tracy's neighbors began looking out their windows. There were sounds of neighborhood dogs barking, as they were tied up. Innocent neighborhood by-standers started watching Tobias. Tracy informed Tobias, he shouldn't look so worried because it's just only concerned neighbors.

Suddenly, Tracy's front door opened wide. An older woman with a splash of grey hair stood in front of the door. Tracy informed her mother; it's me. Also, I brought a friend! The mother looked at Tobias and smiled. She informed them; children come on in! Tobias entered Tracy's residence. The smell of fried chicken, collard greens and mash potatoes were scenting the entire home. Tracy explained to her mother; how Tobias gave her protection from Craig, who had been harassing her to be his girlfriend. Mama notified how thankful she was. Mama fed Tobias dinner. Tobias thought the dinner was the best food ever and felt comfortable in the family's home.

Then, the T.V started playing, while they became entertained with television shows and their interest in small talk.

Excitedly, Tracy's mother influenced Tracy to take Tobias on a tour of the neighborhood. Tobias agreed; but Tracy had to grant Tobias his wish of being escorted out the neighborhood. Then, Tracy's mother greeted Tobias good-bye. Deep down inside, Tobias felt leery of the dangers of Tracy's neighborhood. Tracy comfort Tobias again. She held Tobias hand and assured him everything would be okay. Surprisingly, Tobias felt comfort. For a moment, Tobias forgot he was Tracy's Booty Guard; and his powers had been temporary post pone by another force. The warmth and kindness of Tracy, serenaded Tobias. Tobias began thinking more of romancing than protecting Tracy. They passed by a food truck and a river walk.

Where Tobias lived, was on the city outskirts. So happened, the apartment projects were in walking distance to city attractions. They walk to the neighborhood exit street and passed a food truck with a river walk. Tobias and Tracy sat on a park bench by the river walk and enjoyed lemonade drinks. Tracy informed Tobias; her neighborhood was close to a recreation area with an outdoor swimming pool, which was operated by city workers. Also, libraries and other attractions were close. There was no shortage of attractions and entertainment in the area. The difference with Tobias' neighborhood was folks purchased and delivered their entertainment home or drove far distances away to an establishment. In Tracy's neighborhood, Tobias felt romantic.

As talk progressed on the park bench, Tracy inquired to Tobias; how he was feeling. Tobias had a glazed look in his eye. He rubbed Tracy's right leg softly. Activity in the background suddenly phased out. Tobias heartbeat thumped faster; and he felt warmer inside. He got ready to speak of having a different opinion towards Tracy. Except, two attractive women who were holding hands walked pass them and stopped. Tobias lost thought for a moment. Then, he called his father to pick him up from the neighborhood. Tracy got ready to speak; but Tobias became distracted because the two attractive women began kissing passionately. It appeared to Tobias; everyone was feeling romantic in the area. As Tobias gathered his senses, he noticed from a little distance, Craig and his friends.

Craig and his friends were shouting disruptive words to the two attractive women. They were creating a disturbance, so Tobias began to walk the opposite way. Tracy was not going to allow Craig to disrupt the women's activities. She told Tobias to follow her, while she stopped Craig and his friends from being disruptive. Tobias gave a disbarring look. Although, he followed behind Tracy anyways. Once Tobias reached the situation, Tracy started fussing at Craig. An innocent little stray poodle dog began barking also. Craig and his friends started touching the attractive women. Tracy threw rocks at Craig and his friends. Then, Tobias grabbed Craig and tossed him to the ground. Craig friends tried to help; but Tracy continued to throw rocks at them. Tobias chased Craig away, while Tracy chased Craig's friends away with rocks.

Sadly, Tobias did not stay long afterwards. A disgruntled poodle dog chased Tobias away. The poodle dog did not like all the commotion and felt Tobias was the reason. Luckily, Tobias noticed; his father was waiting in his car for him. Tobias rushed to get inside his father's car with the poodle dog running behind from short distance. Tracy informed Tobias, she was grateful for his protection. Although, shocking to see a little poodle dog would chase Tobias away and not the disruptive boys. Tobias informed, when it came to protect someone's sexual freedom, he supported it. Albeit, a little poodle dog would get involved with the situation. An understanding from Tobias filtered; he was called for duty only to be the Booty Guard. For stray animals, you must notify the Animal control office.

Tobias' father Rogers was not happy with Tobias booty duty service either. Rogers explained he was concerned; Tobias was putting his life in danger. Tobias informed he felt empathy for sexual victims and cried inside his sole. He believed his father could never understand his motives because there was something hidden deep down inside. Tobias never told him; he was a sexual victim too. It made him sick inside to remember the incident which he experienced. Which is why, he knew what he must do for his High School. Since Tobias believed so strongly in his booty guard service, he would start his own social group to spread the word about victims of sexual incidents. No more would Tobias allow his father or anyone who influenced him to overlook sexual offences at his High School.

Therefore, Tobias organized a petition for school students, to prevent teenage sex. This way, students would not be pressured from other students to do sexual encounters. Tobias' cousin Mercedes thought it was a great idea. Mercedes helped create stickers and signs which read, "Prevent teenage sex". The teachers of North City Town High School were highly impressed with the message from Tobias and other students who joined the petition. An after-school rally was conducted which was created by the petitioners. In charge of the petition were Tobias and Mercedes. Therefore, Melvin decided to attend. Then, Ricky showed up. Ricky praised Tobias on how he was able to influence students on a mission. Although, he was not happy with Tobias or the mission.

Tobias was a good football player. He gave up the idea of playing because he spent too much time being the Booty Guard. Ricky attended the rally, for to persuade Tobias to play football again. Tobias and the football players were friends, during the time in Jr. High School. Tobias played a little on the Jr. High School football team. Unfortunately, the Jr. High School football coach named Johnson, placed him on indefinite probation. For unknown reasons, Tobias fought against Coach Johnson's discipline tactics. Although, football players around continued believing; Tobias was good. So, Ricky wanted Tobias to play football again and help the school football team. Ricky's position was running back in Jr. High School. Tobias was a good full back blocker. Together they made a good combination.

Unfortunately, Ricky's reputation as a good football player was becoming slim. Without Tobias' good blocking in the back field, Ricky was only an average football player. Ricky was just a first-year freshman in High School. No respect came to an unproven freshman football player. As an assistant or lobbyist, the quarter back named Rice of the High School football team made a proposition standing beside Ricky. Rice informed to Tobias, if he played on the football team, there want to be any sex victims occurring from football players. This was a welcoming message to Tobias. With the acknowledgement from the school staff and students, Tobias made an agreement to play football again. Tobias became a High School football player for his school in his second year of High School.

During Tobias' second year in High School, North City Town H.S football was outstanding. The football program started better than it did in years. With Rice as quarter back, Ricky as tail back and Tobias as full back, it became the perfect team. Furthermore, Tobias continued his booty guard service but at a minimum. Then, Ricky became distracted with off field activity; and his concentration in football games became poor. Ricky was angry and disgruntled. Sherri, who was Ricky's girlfriend, joined the petitions for prevention of teenage sex. It was concerning to Ricky because he was in a sexual relationship with Sherri for over a year. So, Tobias had a conversation with Ricky. Tobias reassured Ricky; Sherri was only going through a temporary phase in her life. He would talk to Sherri about any concerns she felt against Ricky.

Furthermore, Mercedes followed through with organizing awareness for High School sex victims. The rallies for participation of sex prevention on teenagers drew more support from school administrators. Students participated in rallies by buying signs, tee shirts and clip on pins which read, "Prevent Teenage Sex". Mercedes made speeches and recognized Tobias for the Booty Guard, who served to prevent sex crimes. Although, backlash from school students were heard discreetly. At one Prevent Teenage Sex rally, Tobias told Sherri, teenage sex was only bad when two people don't know each other very well and love is not involved. Although, if there was an understanding through counseling and a commitment by both parties, then teenage sex wouldn't be a problem.

Sherri made amends with Ricky. Although, an ultimatum was created. They would become married, while in High School. Therefore, Sherri and Ricky both became clients of Tobias' booty guard service. Tobias reassured their loyalty to each other. It was an easy job for Tobias because they loved each other gratefully. The booty guard service lasted about 6 months before they married. While the other students at their school, tried to maintain respect of their decisions. Ricky regained his confidence in football play. North City Town H.S started winning games again. Sherri and Mercedes praised Tobias at a rally. At a reception, more fans were generated for Tobias. Teenage sex prevention rallies were going well. Unfortunately, Sherri got pregnant and dropped out of school.

Nevertheless, Tobias heard Sherri obtained a job in the business district of Winston-Salem, NC for reasons to take care of her newborn child. From request by Ricky, Tobias searched for Sherri's employment job. Then, after Tobias and Ricky found out about Sherri's job. They visited Sherri on her job. Sherri was employed at a motel bar in the downtown area called the District. Therefore, Tobias obtained employment at Sherri's job, only to continue his service as Sherri's Booty Guard. Therefore, Ricky and Tobias felt better about Sherri's safety. Although, it was no easy job for Tobias because the District was a tourist place known for criminal activity.

Tobias informed his parents; he would be working in the District as a Motel Security Patrol Officer for the District area. Tobias' father Rogers was no stranger of the rumors about the District. Mr. Rogers knew as a child of killings and muggings which occurred. He also knew the District was safer now because of the City Mayor. Although, ideas of Tobias working in the District still did not change things. Since Tobias was about to be a junior in High School going to the eleventh grade, Mr. Rogers bought Tobias a used Dodge Charger car for transportation for travel to work. He also reminded him to call on a regular basis in times of emergencies. A look of appreciation and gratitude overcame Tobias. Maybe, Mr. Rogers understood Tobias aspirations after all.

The motel bar where Sherri worked, was adjacent to a 4-star motel called W-S Prime. It was operated by a man named Fred Williams. Fred Williams was a middle-age man and grew up with Tobias' father. He trained employees with a zero-tolerance attitude. There was very little compromise and change of agreement with Mr. Williams. Once a person signs an agreement to work for Mr. Williams than you were pretty much obligated to fill your agreement. Unless, if Mr. Williams considered you was unfit to work than he was ready to cancel the contract. It also took someone who Mr. Williams respected and had history with for him to change his decision. Examples were politicians like the City Mayor, Mr. Williams' wife or Tobias' father who possibly could influenced Mr. Williams.

W-S Prime's bar tried to operate a brunch buffet by day; and at night, it teased as an upscale adult entertainment club. The bar tender was among the top in the state and the cooks were graded every year. As the female staff, they were background checked and tested for customer service skills. Great customer service skills were most important to the bar because of the District's reputation. Mr. Williams hired and trained his most trusted security staff to protect his beautiful female employees which gave great hospitality to the motel's guest and customers. This helped the District's reputation, while generating economic impact for the city and keeping Mr. Williams employed. Therefore, Tobias received the security patrol job overwhelmingly because of his passion.

Mr. Williams instantly was attracted to Tobias because of a phone interview. Then, it probably helped Tobias because his daddy was named Mr. Rogers Nelson, who grew up with Mr. Williams. Also, considering Tobias scored excellent on his security test for the job. Tobias work hours were the same as Sherri. On weekdays, Tobias worked 6 pm until 12 pm. Then weekends, it was from 6pm until 2 am. It wasn't difficult for Tobias because football season was over and school was close to ending for the summer. The Motel Security uniform fitted Tobias well and he looked classy in his shiny 5 speed Dodge Shadow automobile. Before Tobias entered the District, he stopped at the top of a hill where he could see the busy traffic in the city.

So happened, the City Mayor issued a police check for weapons at the downtown entrance thruway. It was Tobias first day of work and the police recognized his uniform, when he was stop before entering the thruway. As Tobias received his police check, the person in charge admired his car. Tobias car had a front tag which read, "M.A.C". This was Tobias symbol for himself to represent his first automobile car. The meaning of M.A.C - was my automobile car. Tobias was proud of his daddy and life now. He felt confident; he was headed in the right direction with his life. About the time, Tobias arrived at the loading dock and security room, Sherri across the street was standing in front of the bar entrance. Sherri waved to signal; she was doing fine.

Tobias informed Ricky by his cell phone; Sherri appeared to be fine and he would visit her whenever he finished his brief meeting. Ricky mentioned, he believed Sherri was going to be okay. After Tobias got brief in the meeting, he spoke to Mr. Williams about daily routine details. Mr. Williams informed Tobias, he should make safety checks on the bar at least every other hour. Tobias must wear a radio, baton and handcuffs. Also, he would be making reports daily. Tobias agreed and informed, he was making his first safety check immediately. His first initial safety check started around 6:15 pm. Tobias went out the motel door, then crossed the street and met a hand full of women standing outside. Although, he didn't see Sherri at first.

There was a woman among the group who greeted Tobias. She gave Tobias a strange look and said, "Hello". Tobias could tell she was puzzled to see him. The woman was named Helen. She had on a black blouse and tight-fitting jeans. Therefore, Helen wore the company name tag on her blouse. Her assumptions were Tobias was lost because she didn't recognize him. Simultaneously, Helen informed her group; staff security patrol was here. Tobias announced his name; and he was the new safety patrol officer. He requested to see Sherri. Helen asked Tobias, "Was there a problem and could she help him because she was the supervisor over the woman?" Tobias informed Helen, there was no problem; except, he wanted to speak to Sherri. He recognized Helen made a frown as she retrieved Sherri for him.

Helen who was approximately 5 feet 3 inches tall, made a quick dash to retrieve Sherri. She was supervisor of the female customer service staff inside the bar for over 4 years. At the young age of 20, Helen became supervisor at W-S Prime. Now at the age of 22, Helen felt entitled to ask questions about anything concerning W.S Prime. Helen albeit, she was still young, carried herself mature and classy. She had sexy brown eyes and black hair. Also, she could talk with expertise and could charm most guys in her age bracket. With a college degree in hospitality, plus communications with a top-notch security staff, Mr. Williams had little concern for Helen safety. Curiously but fast, Helen got Sherri's attention and directed towards Tobias.

Sherri informed Helen, she was grateful. The new safety patrol officer was her school friend, wanting to know was she okay. Then, she introduced Tobias to Helen. Helen acknowledge she had introduced herself already. Although, she didn't mind being introduced again. Sherri informed all the women staff; they can rest assured about any doubts in the bar with crime protection because Tobias have a phobia of sex crimes. She acknowledged Tobias had been her booty guard protector and with others, since her eighth-grade school year. He has been recognized in High School from staff, students and peers for his care with certificates and awards. If there was any trouble about to occur from sex, Tobias would be the first to investigate.

Surprisingly, Helen instantly became impressed with Tobias because she was young and had previous problems with sex predators. Also, because W-S Prime's bar made money by selling alcohol and advertising beautiful women on display, which drew sexual predators. It didn't take long, before Helen wanted Tobias to be her personal Booty Guard. Helen loved Tobias broad shoulders and tall built. Tobias well-mannered personality was overwhelming. He was Helen's and the other female staff comforter. There was nothing Helen wouldn't do for Tobias. Furthermore, Tobias in return, made sure the females were happy by making extra rounds when not needed. Tobias tried to make the rounds unnoticeable but Mr. Williams caught glimpse of him making frequent visits with his daughter Helen in the bar.

One day, Tobias overheard from Helen, Sherri was inviting schoolmates to the bar. Furthermore, Sherri was having a party on Tobias day off. Tobias was curious, so he notified Ricky of his knowledge. Ricky informed Tobias, Sherri invited him. Then, he invited Persia. Albeit, time had passed almost 3 years, since Ricky and Persia were together; and Sherri got raped. Still Tobias had bad vibes about Ricky and Persia's conduct together. Especially, when Ricky and Persia drank alcohol; and they both were below the drinking age. Then, they would start making sexual advances at females. Therefore, Tobias intuition occurred; and he decided to be there in the bar. Tobias believed something strange might just happen; and he wouldn't have forgiven himself, if he wasn't there at the bar.

Therefore, Tobias arrived in the W-S Prime motel parking lot on his off day. Nothing seemed unusual. Tobias decided to walk across the street unannounced into the bar. Helen was shocked to find his appearance there but happy. Tobias recognized a slightly deep voice in the far back. Then, he noticed Sherri sitting on someone's lap. It was Ricky's lap; and Persia was running his mouth to another female in the bar. Luckily, neither Ricky nor Persia was drinking alcohol. This would be grounds to call security. Tobias approached Persia slowly. Then, Persia turned around and greeted him. Persia was talking and trying to seduce a female employee. He inquired, how he could get to know the female employee. Instantly, Tobias informed, the female workers were nice looking but for entertainment only.

Persia commenced on introducing himself from one female to the next. Then, Ricky approached him. Tobias informed to Ricky; this place was not a very good place to have a party. Ricky asked Tobias, "Why not?" Tobias informed Ricky, the District area downtown was known for criminal activity. Albeit, the City Mayor had made a public statement of intentions for a family orient city atmosphere in the downtown area. The W-S Prime bar still had a long way to go. It was considered night life entertainment mostly for grown-ups and not young adults. Although, young adults worked in the establishment and were able to attend as long, they did not drink alcohol. Then, Persia walked by Tobias and tried to grab a female employee's hand. Tobias informed Persia, he doesn't touch the female employees.

Persia was intoxicated. Tobias could tell Persia had been previously drinking because he smelled of alcohol. Persia kept repeating inside the bar, he needed him a girlfriend. Helen and Tobias made it a priority to explain to Persia, he was welcome to make small talk with the female staff. Although, Helen informed she would not guarantee, he would find a girlfriend in the bar. Ricky observed Helen and Tobias trying to make Persia see reality. He suggested for them to allow Persia to have some fun. Therefore, Helen sent her best female staff to assist Persia. Finally, Persia calmed down. He began to enjoy himself. Tobias started to feel everything was going to be okay. Then, Ricky and Persia decided to leave the bar.

Tobias and Helen felt relieved to see Ricky and Persia leave. Prior to Persia leaving, Persia thanked the bar staff for their hospitality. Sherri believed Ricky and especially Persia enjoyed themselves. The female staff named Kandis made Persia feel as if he had a real girlfriend inside the bar. She exchanged phone numbers with Persia and informed Persia, he would get special treatment, whenever she sees him inside the bar. Persia unexpectedly informed Tobias, he was in love with Kandis the bar staff. He implied, Kandis was going to be his girlfriend. Although, Tobias did not take Persia's words as serious. Tobias repeated to Persia, the female staff were there for entertainment. The female staff were not there to have personal relationships with clients.

Time passed by, while Tobias life became busy. W-S Prime Motel realized Tobias was one of their best employees. The Winston-Salem Police Department started to notice less crime in the city's downtown area and around the W-S Prime Motel. More awards were given to Tobias for his efforts to control sex crimes at school and work. The City police officers notice Tobias' accomplishments to prevent sex crimes. Popularity came quickly to Tobias. Then, Helen reported a problem with his associate Persia. Persia had been attending the bar on a regular routine. Sadly, he had been stalking Kandis also, during her personal time away from work. Then, he claimed Kandis had stollen his wallet at the bar. Tobias schedule a meeting at the bar with Persia to discuss the accusations, he was making against Kandis.

Tobias met with Persia in front of Helen and the female staff. He informed Persia, his desires to have a relationship with Kandis was strictly in the bar. Also, the relationship would only be him having communication with the woman. It would not turn into a sexual relationship. Furthermore, the staff women were only for entertainment and no one there was going to be his girlfriend. Surprisingly, Helen became offended by Tobias words. Helen asked Tobias confidentially, "Did he really believe the female staff thought clients were business only? Albeit, some staff members do fall in love with their customers". She informed Tobias; she cared a lot for him. Tobias became confused. He thought, he was saying the proper thing to prevent Persia from making sexual advances at the female staff.

Rumors were heard about Persia. Reports in town were Persia was going to shoot everyone in W-S Prime Motel bar. Sherri notified the female staff; the rumors were true. Helen notified Tobias; she was fearful of the rumors. She became worried for her staff. In the Motel parking lot, Tobias began escorting Kandis and Helen from their vehicles to the bar. Tobias wore chest protection armor for emergencies. Kandis informed Tobias; maybe, if she had a sexual relationship with Persia, then threats wouldn't be happening. Tobias notified Kandis; with sexual predators, they don't normally stop with one person. If he was successful with having sex with her, then he would try it on someone else too. Tobias figured; his best hope to stop Persia was with a strong show of defense.

Persia, who was soon to be an eleventh-grade student and a football player at North City Town High School, was well known by Tobias. On the High School football team, Tobias, Ricky and Persia were the best players who were in their Junior class in High School. At the High School, all three football players knew each other well. Their history together became a love and hate affair. The reason was because they were so competitive with each other on the football field and off the football field. Therefore, when Ricky and Persia entered Tobias' workplace, they thought they were going to get special treatment because of their history together. Also, Sherri enticed Ricky and Persia to show up at the bar. Then, Sherri influence Persia into thinking, he was going to find him a girlfriend at the bar.

Persia was a hot head and stubborn; but he was strong as a bull. Persia maybe, stood an inch shorter than Tobias. Both men stood over 6 feet tall. It was clear by their status; they were athletic and strong. Tobias played fullback or halfback and Persia played defensive linebacker. Furthermore, Ricky played tailback. Surprisingly, this was not comforting for Tobias. Although, Tobias and the other guys had momentarily become friends; they still would not listen to his logic. Therefore, Tobias informed the motel manager Mr. Williams of the predicament in the bar. It was Tobias last resort. He was standing outside, observing the view of the bar's front door entrance. Mr. Williams were walking around the motel and noticed Tobias just staring at the bar.

Mr. Williams asked Tobias, "Was he having a lot of problems with the bar because he makes a lot of trips down there?" Tobias informed Mr. Williams; he didn't want any problems to happen to the bar because of something he wasn't doing correctly. Then, Mr. Williams asked Tobias; "Was there something going on, which he needed to share?" Maybe, he had something going on with his daughter Helen because his daughter confided with him on everything about the bar. Tobias admitted; he had been worried too. Then, Mr. Williams instructed Tobias to follow him down to his office. Tobias shook his head and follow Mr. Williams to his office. Once they arrived in Mr. Williams office, Mr. Williams office had a vast number of monitors which he watched.

Mr. Williams had monitors to watch the floors in the motel. The motel consisted of 12 floors, including the annex bar. There were also monitors, which showed the outside area of the motel and bar. Furthermore, there were monitors to observe the city's downtown scene. Tobias looked upon amazement to see so many monitors. His first thought was Mr. Williams was a little extreme with the monitors. Then, he became surprised because of privacy laws. Tobias asked Mr. Williams, "Does the city allows you to use all these monitors?" Mr. Williams informed, why not, it is public knowledge. Anyone can view the city on internet. Then, Mr. Williams began to inform; he realized Tobias have been abandoning his duties at the motel and spending more time at the bar.

Acknowledgement came to Mr. Williams; he was informed, maybe a bond was forming between his daughter and Tobias. Peradventure, Tobias denied the relationship between Helen and him. Although, he did admit concerns for Helen and the other female staff. Furthermore, it was his mistake because his classmate wanted to shoot up the bar. Tobias believed, if there was no history between Persia and him, then Persia wouldn't have arrived at the bar. Mr. Williams informed Tobias; his worries were no more. He occurred evidence which showed Sherri was the cause of Persia acting on the threat. There was a video tape, which Mr. Williams showed on a monitor, where Sherri and Ricky were with Persia in the back seat and being pulled over by city police downtown.

There was a video of Persia, showing him cited for having an unlicensed pistol in his pocket. Therefore, Mr. Williams informed Tobias; the threat of Persia shooting up the bar was over. Tobias felt confident, when he departed Mr. Williams office. He decided to deliver the message at the bar, which the threat of Persia shooting up the bar was over. When Tobias arrived at the bar, Helen and the female staff were working as usual but without Sherri. Tobias figured Sherri must have taken off work because of the incident. Helen informed him; things were back to normal because Persia had been caught and warned about having a pistol in his pocket. Tobias felt enthusiastic about the bar and his job. He began to think about the motel and making his safety rounds.

Tobias stepped outside the bar. Surprisingly, Persia ran quickly around him and entered the bar. Persia held an extended walking stick in his hand. Tobias followed quickly behind him to notify Helen. He shouted to Helen; someone call the police because there is going to be problems. Persia began kicking over tables and chairs and hitting the bar tender with the walking stick. Tobias tried to reach him but female staff were getting in the way. All he heard were things getting broke and the bar tender calling for help. Tobias notified Mr. Williams on his handheld radio of the problem. It took about 5 minutes for police to arrive because they were already roaming in the area. Then, it took another 15 minutes for police to drag Persia out the bar with him wearing handcuffs.

It was a tragedy for Tobias. There was nothing he could do, to make things better. As Tobias returned to school, he got ridiculed for allowing Persia to get arrested during the summertime. Students at North City Town H.S informed Tobias; he was allowing the booty guard duty to go too far. Tobias' father Mr. Rogers explained to him; he was not the police officer or superhero. Tobias at most was a humble security guard, who had a passion for helping sex victims. In addition, he was a High School student, who deserved a teenager boy's life for to accomplish High School. All the worries, which Tobias was taken on in his life, like protecting schoolgirls, club girls, gay boys and making citizen's arrest of sex offenders was not what his father wanted for him.

Peradventure, Tobias had to give up football. Concentrating on preventing sex offenders, took a toll on Tobias. The football players started making fun of Tobias and he hated Coach Johnson the football coach. Coach Johnson would make offensive comments like don't be playing football like a girl or if you make a good play, then the girls will think you are a real man. To Tobias, comments like this was unnecessary. Decidedly, Tobias did not play no more football. Tobias quit football because he wanted to make better grades in school. He also got tired of Coach Johnson's offensive remarks because he had a mission for helping sex victims. It was unfortunate, which Persia was suspended from the team and Ricky had to carry the bulk of the workload for the football team.

Therefore, Tobias continued to work and attend High School. Mr. Williams was grateful because Tobias did not listen to his father's concerns. Mr. Williams promised Tobias, he would teach Tobias all the training needed for helping sex victims. Now, it had become to Tobias desire, passion and dream to be working for the Crisis Unit on sex victims for the City Police. Although, Mr. Williams told him, he had to be focus on other security needs as well. Tobias understood Mr. Williams needs; but he was not too concern. Needless, Tobias found a pretty woman in her middle forties, sitting on a bench on the motel property. The woman was a regular visitor but never paid for a motel room. It appeared to Tobias; she was in some need. So, Tobias asked the woman, "Can he help her?". She replied, "Nope, I am good".

Tobias realized he must make more visual checks of the outside motel property. Another day, the woman was sitting on the bench with a motel guest. The motel guest was a traveling man on business. The man was tall, wearing casual clothes and walked methodically. He and the woman left together in the motel. The activities of the woman sitting on the bench, meeting a man and disappearing became routine. Tobias spoke to the woman and she informed him; he better leaves her alone because she was not bothering anybody. The routine, where she sits on the park bench and disappear with a man continued for about a month. Then, one day, the woman was dressed in high heel shoes, a pretty dress and dress hat. Tobias recognized her, so he gave her a compliment.

The pretty lady just cried. Tobias asked the lady, "What was wrong?" The lady implied as if Tobias should have known what was wrong. Tobias informed, if she was in trouble, he could provide security. Then, a man who was a guest, suddenly arrived. The man, then decidedly, walked away; and Tobias became puzzled. Therefore, he finally informed the Manager Mr. Williams. After a little time, Mr. Williams informed Tobias to ignore the woman and her concerns, unless she makes a complaint. Tobias tried to ignore the incident. Although, soon, he began finding advertisement papers soliciting prostitution at the motel property. Therefore, Tobias made a security round of the entire area and found flyers of advertising prostitution at the bar and the motel area.

Tobias grabbed a flyer and informed the woman on the bench about the flyer. The woman looked at the flyer unfazed. She proclaimed she didn't participate with making the flyers. Tobias informed the woman; he was notifying Mr. Williams of the situation. Mr. Williams only informed Tobias and other staff to be alert for misconduct on the motel property. On another day, Tobias spotted 2 men occupying time in the motel lounge with women in provocative attire. The 2 women were socializing with the woman on the bench. Also, the 2 women were soliciting men in the motel. Tobias noticed motel customers were staring at the 2 women. The 2 women were causing a distraction; so, Tobias called the police. Unfortunately, the 2 women had to be obtained in custody by police.

Then, the 2 men approached Tobias in the lobby. The 2 men asked Tobias, "Why did he call the police on the 2 women?" They were angry and made sure Tobias noticed the flyers, which were posted all over the motel areas about sex for sale. Tobias figured they must be the ones who were responsible for the flyers being posted. Tobias notified Mr. Williams on his radio of the 2 angry men. Mr. Williams advised Tobias to escort the 2 men away from the motel property. The 2 men began threatening Tobias and informed, something bad was going to happen to him. The woman who sat on the bench spoke about the 2 men threatened her life as well, unless she had sex with them. Tobias notified the police again. The 2 men got arrested; but the police allowed the woman to remain on the bench.

Confused, Tobias walked over to the woman on the bench and informed her; he will be her Booty Guard. She didn't have to worry anymore. Although, she should be spending her time somewhere else besides on the bench. The woman informed, her sitting on the bench was part of her life. She was not allowed to go because she had a job to maintain. The woman had a list of names and her cell phone in her hands. She described her list as a clientele list. Nostalgia was her name; and she claimed of being an online saleswoman. Tobias, then informed Mr. Williams of Nostalgia's activities; but surprisingly, Mr. Williams wasn't too concerned. However, Tobias guaranteed the woman's safety anyways. Then, he made his security rounds to the bar.

Once he entered the bar, he told Helen about the woman on the bench. Helen became irate and notified him, he must do his job and remove the woman from the motel property. She informed Tobias; he knows trespassing is against the motel policies. If the woman on the bench was not a paying customer, then she is trespassing. Tobias nodded in agreement; but he told Helen, her father thinks it wasn't a concern. In addition, the police weren't concerned either. Helen promised, if Tobias don't remove the woman from the motel property, then trouble will surely happen. Also, she notified Tobias; Sherri had invited more of her classmates to the bar and has met Melvin and his cousin Mercedes. Helen informed Tobias, he has some interesting associates.

When Tobias returned home, he told his parents of the activities, which occurred in the motel area. Tobias parents advised him to quit the motel job because of the danger. Also, because he needed to concentrate on a life after High School. A notification from Tobias occurred for his parents, which he planned to apply for a city police officer after High School. Time as a junior in North City Town High School were going fast. It was a lot he wanted to accomplish before then. Tobias hoped to have made his school a safer place. He also hoped to have made the District safer as well. Although, Mr. Rogers doubted Tobias ability as a Booty Guard, and Mr. Williams credibility as an honest businessman.

Eagerly, Tammy met with Tobias at school to ask him; if he was still her Booty Guard. If so, then she did not recognize it. It was because Tobias had been so busy with work and clients. There at school, Tobias known clients were Melvin, Mercedes, Ricky and Sherri. Then, at work Tobias kept the female bar staff safe including Helen and Nostalgia, who was the lady on the bench. Nevertheless, he still met Tracy in the projects sometimes, when she needed him. Finally, he couldn't neglect his schoolwork, and his promise to learn how to help sex victims. Peradventure, Tammy was becoming neglected. Tobias plate had become full. He had no time for foolish games because he believed serious issues were happening; regardless, if his father trusted he was doing the right things or not.

Therefore, Tammy made it a mission to visit Tobias at work. When Tammy arrived at Tobias job, peculiar eyes were staring at the motel because Tammy acted like they were lovers, instead of friends. Also, she acted feisty and loud, which was her normal self. Mr. Williams observed her, with thought of his daughter's feelings for Tobias. He made a mental note of Tammy's behavior because he thought she could be Tobias' girlfriend. Nostalgia also witnessed Tammy and believed she was Tobias' girlfriend. It was clear to Tobias; Tammy still had love interest for him. Tammy informed she missed his attention. Then, she claimed to be making more visits because Sherri worked at the bar and the motel appeared to be a nice place.

On one night, while Tobias was on duty, a party was held at the bar. Unknown attendees were guarding the bar entrance. The attendees carried metal detectors to prevent any weapons from entering the building. Tobias notified he was part of motel security. Although, it seemed to Tobias, motel security had no priority. The attendees informed him; he had to receive approval from Helen or the party host. Fortunately, a sign was posted with the party host's name at the bottom. The name read "Melvin Reed as Party Host". Therefore, Tobias called Melvin simultaneously, as a person in drag entered the bar. Melvin answered the phone and spoke in a sensual, seductive voice. Melvin informed Tobias, now he wants to contact him because he had been trying to reach him.

Melvin notified Tobias, he had booked the bar for a gay party and needed personal booty guard protection. Football players have been harassing him because he is openly gay. Also, they believe he has favoritism with Tobias; and the High School football players are upset with Tobias. Some of the football players believed, they have a losing football team because Persia was on probation from playing High School sports. The football players said, "Tobias was at fought for reason, Persia was not playing". They wanted to see Tobias and his friends become miserable because they are miserable with the High School football team. Nevertheless, the football players knew about his party and they planned on destroying the event. Tobias comforted Melvin and informed Melvin; he will always be his protector.

CHAPTER 3

Emergence

ONCE MELVIN ARRIVED AT THE bar, Tobias escorted Melvin inside the bar. Inside the bar, Tobias recognized schoolmates. There was Sherri working; and then, Mercedes, Tammy and others were there also. Helen was assisting in the background. Somehow, Nostalgia was able to sneak inside too. Tobias never witness a gay event. The gay party had female impersonators singing and acting. Impersonators pretended to be Diana Ross, Whitney Houston, Tina Turner and others. The show was colorful with great big neon lights. Guest were wearing drag queen attire. The food was exotic and the drinks were expensive. An atmosphere of curiosity was in the air, which made Tobias feel puzzled. So, Tobias stayed motionless for a while.

On the performing stage, there was a singing contest for the participants. Surprisingly, the winner was a female impersonator, who impersonated Madonna. This was the main attraction because Melvin showed favoritism towards the contestant. Then, it turned out, it was Coach Johnson the football coach. Tobias was shocked to witness the football coach as Madonna because the football coach's voice was identical to the singer and his makeup was gorgeous. Tobias tried not to stare and bring attention to himself. Although, overwhelmingly, the coach got the audience's approval. After Tobias observed Melvin and the football coach hugging, he believed Melvin was going to be okay; and he began to relax.

Then, Tobias noticed Sherri answering her cell phone and opening the bar door. As Sherri returned to the bar counter, Ricky and Persia was walking beside her. Tobias stood up and assumed it was going to be trouble. Then, a door attendant back up inside from the bar entrance door. Shockingly, more football players walked inside the bar. Tobias lowered his head in despair. Sherri ran on the performing stage and announced, "There was an announcement to be said, by her boyfriend named Ricky". Both Ricky and Persia walked on the performing stage. First, Ricky looked at the audience. Then, he said, "To my friend Melvin and Tobias. We are one family at North City Town High School. Although, when someone disrupts the family, things have to be done to fix the problem".

Persia informed to the audience, tonight the problem was going to be fix because they were going to celebrate together like old times. Therefore, rather your gay, straight or if you have a relationship phobia, North City Town High School was going to be one big family. However, Persia was going through counseling, while on probation from the football team to control his problems. So, they asked, "Where was Tobias" because they wanted Tobias to make a speech? Tobias slowly, walked up on the performing stage and informed the audience, thank you. Tobias thanked everyone for having a peaceful party. At the end of the night, the football players left quietly, Tobias friends left with peace and the bar closed on time.

Luckily, Tobias and other attendees escorted party goers to their vehicles because outside people were threatening performers. Then, Tobias recognized Melvin and Mr. Johnson holding hands leaving. Tobias started thinking about Mr. Johnson molesting him when he was in the eighth grade. He shouted to Melvin, for him to wait. Nevertheless, Mr. Johnson drove away with Melvin inside. Quickly, Tobias decided to call Melvin and explain for him not to do anything regretful. Melvin informed Tobias, he could relax. He didn't need advice from the Booty Guard. Melvin didn't understand, why Tobias felt concern. Tobias cried and informed Melvin; he molested me. Please don't do nothing strange with Mr. Johnson because he molested me.

Melvin notified Tobias, he knew Mr. Johnson and Tobias had a sexual encounter but he thought it was consensual. Tobias informed, no way! Mr. Johnson made him do it for the team. Mr. Johnson was gay and the football team knew it. He expressed his relationship preference to the football team. Then, Mr. Johnson told the football team; he enjoyed a guy's company because he liked to be pampered by a man. Tobias and team players frowned. He informed Mr. Johnson, a man pampering another man was sickening. Then, he threw up. Therefore, Mr. Johnson became offended and notified Tobias; he would pay for his actions. Furthermore, when he heard the football players make fun of him, he threatened to get rid of them or make it difficult for them in school.

Tobias felt sadden for his football team players. Mr. Johnson preyed on the football players. It became a mission for Tobias to end all sexual misconduct, while he found Mr. Johnson trying to have sexual intercourse with the football players and including making sexual advances at him. Nevertheless, Tobias agreed to allow Mr. Johnson to have a sexual encounter with him. Which Tobias hoped, it would end the predatory actions of Mr. Johnson. Albeit, it became a mental problem for Tobias because it caused him to have a relationship phobia. Tobias was afraid of having sexual intimacy with anyone. He was confused and scared for others including himself, who was not sure about sexual encounters. Therefore, Tobias protected all things, which did not fully trust the concept of sex.

Sadly, Melvin asked Tobias, "Did he go all the way with sex for Mr. Johnson?" Tobias informed he only had a sexual encounter. Then, Melvin mention it would have been okay, for Tobias to have gone all the way. Tobias informed why, when he doesn't like men attractively. He like woman but had difficulty having sex with them. Surely, if he couldn't have sex with women, he wasn't about to have sex with a man. Tobias cared for Melvin; although, he wasn't about to encounter sex with him. Melvin notified Tobias, sex is romantic and fun. You only need to allow yourself to experience the joy which sex could bring. Tobias informed Melvin, he has tried a sexual encounter with a man; and he didn't enjoy it. Tobias claimed he almost passed out from nauseating.

Melvin informed Tobias, he hoped jealousy was not an issue because he loved him. If he would be his private Booty Guard and not worry about protecting anybody else, they could be together. Tobias notified Melvin; he can be with whomever he chooses because he was not gay. He was only trying to warn Melvin; which Mr. Johnson was a sex molester. Melvin sarcastically informed Tobias; he will do anything to enjoy himself, including having sex with Mr. Johnson. Tobias reacting calmly, put his phone back in his pocket and checked on the motel rooms. By accident, Tobias bumped into Nostalgia on a room floor. Tobias first instinct was to stop her. Tobias was upset. So, he asked Nostalgia, "Why are you here on this floor?"

A man came out of a motel room and smiled at Nostalgia. Then, he frowned at Tobias and reentered his motel room. Tobias told Nostalgia; he was warning her not to be soliciting men. If she had decided to prostitute in the motel, then he couldn't promise booty guard protection. Tobias informed Nostalgia; repercussions were going to happen, if she jeopardizes his job. Then, Mr. Williams unknowingly came up from the stair well. Tobias informed Nostalgia; she must hide quickly before Mr. Williams find her there. So, Nostalgia entered the man's room, who came out smiling at her. Nostalgia was able to hide, before Mr. Williams could discover her on the floor. Therefore, Tobias began talking to Mr. Williams. Strangely, Mr. Williams were acting as if he lost something.

Mr. Williams asked Tobias, "He had discovered anything unusual?" Tobias informed he didn't believe he had. Mr. Williams notified Tobias, how about the guest around here. Tobias notified, yes! Oh, yes! Men in women's attire, who are impersonating famous women. Mr. Williams informed Tobias, he thought Tobias had a fear of sexual misconduct. Therefore, if Tobias did have a fear. Then, he was preventing nothing because the freaks were out; and surely, they were going to do some freaky things. Tobias ended his shift. He left feeling strange and uncertain because his night started positive but ended without closure. Nevertheless, gays or straights, he felt the same way. They should have sex on a for needed basis.

Tobias junior year in High School passed quickly. He stayed busy being the Booty Guard for students in school and staff at the motel. Parents of Tobias wanted Tobias to be a normal student. One day, while Tobias was going to school, Tammy was standing outside his window. Tammy's eyes were wandering as if she was checking the entire surroundings. Then, she looked up at Tobias' bedroom window; and Tobias was staring right at her. Tammy informed Tobias; she was sorry if she inconveniences him, but this was their senior year and the prom would soon be coming up. Tobias notified her; he had been thinking about it too. The reason he was thinking about it, was because his parents wanted him to do normal school stuff.

Tammy informed Tobias, since she had no significant other, would he be her prom date. Tobias notified Tammy, as long she was thinking of him as a friend and not expect him to be a boyfriend because prom night added pressure on students to have sex. Besides Tobias figured he couldn't have sex anyways. He was a role model for students in High School. Tobias had been nominated for the most influential student in school. Posters were held high in school to fight teenage sex. Tammy notified Tobias; she understood about his campaign and phobia. She was an advocate for his campaign also. Although, Tobias was Tammy's Booty Guard. How easy it would be for her to prevent from having sex, if she had the Booty Guard as her date.

Tobias claimed it was early, but most likely he would be her prom date because he had to make his parents happy. Therefore, he told his parents; he was going to the prom and already had a date. Tobias' parents asked him, "Who was she?" Tobias informed his parents; her name was Tammy and she was a girl residing in the neighborhood. Tobias brother Reggie was very happy. Reggie figured his job of ending Tobias' phobia had ended. He informed Tobias; he was so happy he doesn't have a sex phobia anymore because everyone knows on prom night sex occurs. Tobias notified Reggie; he wasn't about to have sex with anybody. Besides he was a role model for his campaign to prevent teenage sex. Reggie tried to convince Tobias; if romance was in the air, maybe he would try sex.

As Reggie observed Tobias; he slowly shook his head as to show sympathy. Tobias immediately informed Reggie; he doesn't start feeling sorry for him because he feels, it was the right thing to do. It was not as if he was a virgin. Sex life is not just his cup of tea. Then, Reggie told Tobias; he was moving out and staying with his girlfriend because she was pregnant. Reggie informed Tobias; he worries about him. Tobias notified Reggie; don't worry because he was about to have his own family. Therefore, allow his worries to be for what's to come and remember when he has a child to protect them from sexual encounters, before they become a sex victim or have sex phobias at an early age. Reggie shook his head. Then, he informed to Tobias; hopefully, love will find you brother.

It was Tobias Senior year in High School. As Tobias left for school, he felt emerged to continue his campaign on teenage sex prevention. Tobias decided to observe the school by walking through the area. He was shock to notice; Melvin was holding hands and kissing a boy, who wasn't Mr. Johnson. Then, he found Persia making cat calls at cheerleaders. Last, Tracy still needed his booty guard service from Craig. Ricky tried to shake Tobias hand. Tobias shook Ricky's hand uncertainly. Tobias informed to Ricky, anybody has learned, what he has been trying to prevent. Mercedes tried to reassure Tobias, which everything was going to be okay. Nevertheless. Tobias shouted to everyone, he believed everyone was acting inappropriate.

Mercedes asked Tobias, "What was his problem?" Tobias shook his head disgustedly. He thought Mercedes was wearing a provocative attire. Mercedes was wearing tight jeans and a tight sweater. Tobias informed to Mercedes; how was he going to stop her from becoming a sex victim, when she wears clothes as this? How was he going to stop Melvin from becoming a sex victim, when he acts as if he can give his body away to any guy? How was he going to stop becoming the booty guard and be a regular student, when Tracy is still being harassed by Craig? Mercedes informed to Tobias; he must control his compassion because people have their own opinion about things. Furthermore, no one can save the world or a High School.

Clearly, Tobias was frustrated. An idea came to Tobias. One person couldn't save the world; so, Tobias talked to the school administration. They decided to add stricter laws regarding school wear and conduct. North City Town High School organized another rally to show how small changes with individuals could make a big difference overall. The school hired booty guard monitors for areas, where students socialized the most on school property. They added a sex prevention class for the High School students to informed them about the dangers of casual sex. The atmosphere and conduct of students started to make a change. Teachers and staff recognized Tobias again for his hard work as the Booty Guard. Tobias felt good about himself, despite how other students felt.

It was a control issue for Tobias. The fear of sex, controlled Tobias' mind. Tobias wondered if things could have been different for him, if the school had the new changes in place when Mr. Johnson molested him. The thought of the school acquiring the best defense against sex, reassured Tobias. Therefore, Tobias daydreamed his school was perfect. There were no sex offenders in his school. All the teachers, staff and students conducted themselves professionally. The students wore a black jumpsuit, to cover their body and everybody was a virgin. Tobias would talk among students and they would discuss school stuff only. Furthermore, the students wouldn't worry about dating or sex. Finally, the prom people would be eating, drinking and not dancing close. Lastly, no sex after the prom.

A smile appeared on Tobias face, as Mercedes walked and passed him. Mercedes informed Tobias; she hoped he was happy because all the students were living as prisoners in school. New requirements at North City Town High School had enforced no interacting between opposite sex unless chaperone by a school staff member. Designated school attire was implemented and after school social events were almost eliminated. The school students' entire demeanor had change. They were on the edge because booty guards were watching. Students became fearful of making mistakes in their conduct. The feeling which your conduct was monitored all the time made Mercedes miserable. Tobias acknowledged he appreciated High School now because he was comfortable.

When Tobias returned to work, he noticed more flyers advertising prostitution. It appeared he could not destroy enough flyers before they would be posted again in the motel lobby bathrooms. Therefore, he notified the police. Mr. Williams approached him about his complaint. Tobias requested for Mr. Williams to check the cameras because someone keeps posting flyers. Mr. Williams informed Tobias; he does not worry, soon the culprit who was posting illegal propaganda, was going to be found. Nevertheless, Tobias made a safety round on the motel and spotted Nostalgia on the outside bench. Nostalgia was sitting on a flyer. Tobias began to reassure Nostalgia. He informed Nostalgia; she be on alert for anyone who proposition her to prostitute and notify him quickly.

Nostalgia glanced at him. She told him; he was wasting his time because the city is corrupted. As long the motel manager advertised pretty girls, alcohol with nighttime entertainment in the bar, then the wrong interpretation will come to corrupt individuals. Nostalgia guessed, the motel manager would probably have to close the bar and make it a dining facility only. Tobias informed Nostalgia; he will go and talk to Helen, the staff manager. As Tobias recommends to Helen about ending alcohol sales and nighttime entertainment, she propositions Tobias to become more than her Booty Guard. Helen wanted Tobias to be her boyfriend. She asked Tobias, "Would he take her to where her father was located?" Then, they can negotiate with her father about the bar.

As Tobias and Helen walked to Mr. Williams motel office, Helen informs Tobias; she was a lonely woman and needs a companion to start a family. Helen advised Tobias; the motel was a great place to work for. In the motel industry, there were a lot of jobs and the benefits were good. Furthermore, Mr. Williams has made a comfortable life for her and a companion. If Tobias would consider partnering with her, then he could live a prosperous life too. Tobias was caught off guard by Helen remarks. He began to tell her about his aspirations. Then, they met Mr. Williams, while he informed Tobias; good help was hard to find, especially someone which everybody gets along with. Helen has eyes for him. She needs a boyfriend, who can give her a good time and make her happy.

Tobias explained to Mr. Williams; his desires was for the motel to be safe from sexual predators. Maybe, adding restrictions for check-in time and no alcohol sales on motel property. Install more outside lights and a roving motor vehicle for the outside motel area. Also, Tobias wanted motel security to be trained by City Police in the victims' unit. This way, motel security would have a better understanding of sex victims. Mr. Williams informed he would try to make more updates and changes in the motel. Although, he wasn't making any changes drastically because he had obligations to host parties. North City Town High School had booked the motel bar for the after-Prom party. Then, the City Mayor hosted the Galilee Ball event in the bar area.

Frustration came upon Tobias in Mr. Williams office. He knew it probably meant more drinking events, security patrols and stress on him. Therefore, Tobias smacked the top of Mr. Williams' copy machine uncontrollably. Surprisingly, Tobias spotted a flyer on top of the copy machine which advertised, "One-night with reasonable fee of passionate love with a beautiful lady at W – S Prime Motel". Tobias glanced at the flyer. Then, he told Mr. Williams, this is what gives him headaches. Someone was posting the flyers up in the motel and causing a lot of trouble. Mr. Williams shook his head and informed Tobias; he knew already and was monitoring the problem with cameras. Then, Helen grab Tobias arm and took him to her private room in the motel.

Inside Helen's private motel room was a suite with adjoining bedrooms with a lounge and kitchenette. Instantly, Tobias became impressed. Although, her lounging area was a great big office desk, where she kept files on her staff members. Also, the lounge area smelled like an emporium because she had assorted flowers station periodically. As Helen was discussing the business, when they entered the room, Tobias smelled the flowers because they attracted his attention. Helen notified Tobias, the motel business has a reputation to its customers; and although, change was good, it must be gradual changes. So, customers shouldn't become too disappointed by the differences of the past. Then, she took Tobias on a tour of her room.

Helen showed Tobias the kitchenette. The kitchenette had a stove, refrigerator and sink. Tobias asked Helen, "Did she do much cooking?" Helen informed she cooked a little. However, her expertise wasn't cooking. Besides, the motel rooms had food delivery service; and Helen enjoyed their food. Therefore, Helen thought her best skills were operated in the bedroom. This was her Prime years for mating; and Helen had been waiting for the right person. Now, Helen had Tobias where she wanted him, in her motel room. So, she was going to let him know about her real talents. Helen took him inside her bedroom, where the lights was off. Then, she cut the lights on and showed Tobias the bed. Tobias looked in amazement.

"What in God's name!" Tobias screamed in amazement. Helen had chains hanging above her bed. Then, she had a display full of sex toys. Tobias asked Helen, "You use these sex toys?" Helen informed she did because it helped her sex become spicy and interesting. Tobias informed he had to use her bathroom and threw up. Next, he returned and notified; he rather not had to think about her sex toys. Helen told Tobias; his friends notified her of his sexual relationship with a man and perhaps, he enjoys a man's private area next to him. Therefore, she had purchased a variety of dildoes and vibrators for his choice. Tobias returned to the bathroom and threw up again. After he finished, Tobias notified Helen, he was leaving because of something highly important he must tell Mr. Williams.

Tobias decided to step outside for some fresh air to register, what had occurred before talking to Mr. Williams. He hated he became sick from seeing the sex toys. Helen looked sexy, staring into his eyes and showing her office space. The thought of living in a motel with a beautiful woman and having a career seem like a fairy tale to Tobias. Albeit, his beliefs and phobias stopped him from fantasizing about having any motel romance. Besides, Tobias wanted a career helping sex victims and refused to be caught again by the influence of sex. The Booty Guard was who he was and not some gigolo or sex boy. Tobias figured his job was to prevent freaky sex acts as this. Furthermore, he wasn't a gigolo or sex toy. Then, he noticed Nostalgia sitting on the bench.

Therefore, Tobias greeted Nostalgia with a hello. Tobias became puzzled because she was dressed seductively. He informed Nostalgia; she looked nice and needed to be careful while dressed like this, when sitting alone for a lone time because men might interpret reasons to do evil things. Nostalgia informed Tobias; since he was concerned, would he be the one who might do evil things. So, Tobias notified he was concerned because it was his duty to worry about her safety. Then, Nostalgia told Tobias; she had forgot, he was not only security but the Booty Guard who wants to help sex victims. Furthermore, if this was so true, why he hadn't reported the police about Mr. Williams because he was the cause of sexual assaults in the motel. Tobias asked Nostalgia, "What was she talking about?"

Nostalgia stared into Tobias' eyes with sarcasm; but she was also seductive. It was ironic to Tobias because he got this same look from someone else but couldn't remember from who. Nostalgia was wearing this long tight-fitting black dress with a low cleavage and high heel shoes. The dress made her look a little younger than her normal look. Tobias informed her; she must not like Mr. Williams. Although, Mr. Williams appeared to be trying to make security a priority. Nostalgia informed Tobias; he needs to observe how the female staff are dressed and the male establishment who frequently stay in the motel. She notified Tobias; the motel has guest who focus on buying sex. Decidedly, Tobias headed for Mr. Williams office to discuss some terms with him.

Once Tobias arrived at Mr. Williams' office, he witnessed additional copies of advertisement posters on a shelf soliciting female sex. Tobias assumed Mr. Williams was recovering the posters from areas, where the posters had been displayed and were not wanted. Peradventure, he wasn't sure. Nevertheless, Tobias informed Mr. Williams, he must had found more unwanted posters displaying in the motel. Mr. Williams cleared his throat and declared; motel activity has become a real problem. Therefore, he had decided to make Tobias, manager of security. Tobias became flattered; but he denied the position. He informed Mr. Williams; this was not what he wanted. What he wanted, was to train and help sex victims. Then, apply for a position after High School with the Police force.

Mr. Williams was very disappointed. Although, he kind of knew, where Tobias' heart was at. Then, Mr. Williams decided to inform Tobias about the City's Galilee Ball, where the Mayor, police officers, firemen and other city workers would be honored for their efforts in the community. Mr. Williams promised, he would give a good reference to the Chief of Police about how Tobias would make a good police officer for the Preventive Victims Enforcement Unit. Although, there was one stipulation, Tobias would have to work during the High School Football Convention and the City Mayor's Galilee. Tobias was concerned about working the High School Football Convention because he was once a football player; and he knew of football players who would love to make his job difficult.

Decidedly, Tobias agreed to the terms of Mr. Williams; and Mr. Williams agreed to help Tobias. Therefore, he was satisfied. Now, he became concerned about the accusations of Nostalgia. So, he asked Mr. Williams, "What can he do to stop the prostitution in the motel?" Mr. Williams informed Tobias; you don't jeopardize your safety for any woman. A hooker is going to be a hooker regardless. You mainly notify me the owner; and I will take care of it. Tobias once again became frustrated with the prostitution because Mr. Williams wasn't concern. He didn't know who to talk with. Therefore, Tobias discussed the problem with Helen. As soon, Tobias mention prostitution, Helen spoke of Nostalgia's name.

Helen informed Tobias, he must have caught Nostalgia in the motel. Tobias told Helen, he hasn't visually seen Nostalgia prostituting in the motel; but it appeared, she was soliciting men a few times. Helen informed Tobias; Nostalgia is her mother. Also, Nostalgia has part ownership of the motel. Mr. Williams and Nostalgia are divorced; even-though, they maintain an agreement. Therefore, Mr. Williams and herself tolerates Nostalgia; but she has an understanding not to cause issues with the motel. Now, Tobias understood. Then, Tobias became confused again. The thought of Nostalgia being married to Mr. Williams. It was too surprising to Tobias. Tobias started thinking about how sexy Nostalgia looked. He thought about Helen. Helen did look like Nostalgia. They both were sexy.

As Tobias returned home from a hard night of work, he informed his father, Mr. Williams offered him a management security job. Also, Tobias informed his parents, about the dangers of prostitution activities happening in the motel. Tobias' father Mr. Nelson was furious. Mr. Nelson hoped Tobias would not accept the job position. He informed Tobias; motel security was too much of a responsibility for a teenage child, who was a senior in High School. Besides his priorities should only be about High School. Then, Mr. Nelson informed Tobias; he didn't trust Mr. Williams or the City Mayor's promise of turning the District into a more family friendly area. Also, something was not adding up with Mr. Williams, his ex-wife and daughter. Why was prostitution going on inside the motel?

However, Tobias returned to school and found everything operating the way he wanted, which was smoothly. Students were attending class as regular students. No one was socializing, so they were not happy. Tobias figured it was because football season was over; and the football players started looking for other activities to keep them occupied. A euphoria was in the atmosphere with the Senior students. Once winter was over, it was a time to concentrate on life after graduation. In between time, they had the Football convention and After Prom party to attend. Tobias received a phone call from Tracy. She needed him to give her the booty guard service because Craig felt a need to harass her again. Therefore, Craig got a visit by Tobias.

Craig loved muscle cars. Tobias had one of the finest muscle cars in school. There were few North City Town H.S students who knew about Tobias' car. So, Tobias parked in the school parking lot, while he waited on the inside for Craig. Tobias sunk deep down on the floor of his automobile to hide from Craig. The school front door opened, Craig came out and noticed the Dodge car with the M.A.C tag on front. Craig began talking to another student by Tobias car. He shouted, "Oh wee, what a fine fanny car here!" Tobias raised up. He spoke out loud to Craig, "You like going around, looking at peoples' fannies. You look at Tracy's fanny and now, you like my car's fanny. I think you are a booty hole looker".

There was no hesitation with Tobias, as he got out his vehicle and grab Craig by the neck. Craig pleaded with Tobias. He had spoken, he was a fellow football player and teammate. They didn't have to fight because they were teammates. Tobias informed Craig, he didn't play football anymore or games with him. It was time for him to have learned a lesson. Craig was choking to death. Then, someone alerted Mr. Johnson the football coach. Mr. Johnson ran to meet Tobias. He informed Tobias; the Booty Guard was supposed to serve the students and protect the victims. It was not to injure the predator. Therefore, the predator would become the victim; and the protector would start preying on the predator. Nevertheless, Tobias came to his senses and stopped choking Craig.

Then, a long conversation happened between Craig and Tobias. An understanding occurred, which Craig had an affection for Tracy but didn't know how to express it properly. So, Tobias told Craig, how to properly attract girls. One easy way was Craig changed his personality to impress Tracy. Craig stopped harassing Tracy and treated her with kindness. He then, befriended her and became her Booty Guard. Tracy enjoyed it; and they started going on dates. Surprisingly, Tracy trusted Craig enough to become his date for Prom night. Initially, Tobias was satisfied because Tracy had someone else as the Booty Guard. Furthermore, Tobias acquired a friend and a companion to stop the sexual assaults at North City Town H.S.

For some Seniors in High School, the Prom was thought to be the highlight in their High School career. Although, if you are the Booty Guard, it could be stressful. Not only did Tobias have to make sure his date Tammy was happy at the Prom, but he had to take his enthusiasm to his job. There, they were preparing for the After-Prom party. Tobias did not notify anyone at the motel until late, he was attending the Prom. He didn't want anyone at the motel to be making jokes about Prom night. So, Tobias kept it a secret, until a week before the ceremony. Furthermore, Tammy wanted to surprise him with a free meal at a restaurant. Sherri promised Tammy, W-S Prime motel bar would give her a discount on dinner before the Prom. No one knew, Tobias was going on a date at the Prom.

The day of the Prom, Tobias picked Tammy up in his Dodge Shadow car. Tobias and Tammy were both dressed in Prom attire. Tammy notified Tobias, she wanted to surprise Tobias with dinner at the W-S Prime bar because Melvin and Sherri were there. They were going to the Prom too. Tobias had mix emotions at first because it was at his job. He didn't want to arrive at his job, when he had time off. However, since he had more classmates there waiting on them, he felt obligated to attend. As soon, Tobias and Tammy walked through the bar's front entrance, Sherri escorted them to a group table. Sherri notified the classmates; Ricky and she were attending the Prom also. Everyone at the table appeared to be in good spirits because of the Prom. It began as a happy time for Tobias.

Tobias was proud to find; Melvin had his prom date at the group table and he wasn't talking about seeing Mr. Johnson. Persia arrived and he was talking respectfully with his date Mercedes. Unbelievably, he managed to influence Mercedes; and now, they were going to the Prom. Then, Tracy and Craig showed at the bar. Tracy looked so beautiful to Tobias; he almost became a little jealous. Soon, Ricky started making jokes about a Booty Guard. The joke was, there were no need for Booty Guard services because everyone was happy and not disgruntled. Then, right after everyone's food arrived, Tobias experienced a tap on his shoulder. The cook informed Tobias; his booty guard service was needed in the kitchen.

Tobias became confused. Who would need the booty guard service in the kitchen? Tobias walked in the kitchen. It was Helen with her arms folded and angry. Helen spoke, Tobias needed booty guard service for himself because she was going to kick his booty. She informed Tobias; he should have asked her to be his Prom date first. Albeit, Helen thought he wasn't the Prom type. This because Tobias told her he didn't like parties; albeit, someone will always spike the punch with alcohol. Helen reminded Tobias, after the Prom, it was normally drinking and sex. Therefore, he would probably have sex with a High School girl, who can't do for him what she can. Tobias informed Helen, his entire purpose would be to protect individuals from having unwanted sex and be on booty guard duty.

The Prom was a glamorous event. Inside the event center were decorations with balloons and signs advertising North City Town H.S Prom. High School students were dressed in their finest attire and jammed pack in one area for excitement and entertainment. There was a local Disc Jockey playing music at a table for everyone's enjoyment. The buffet table had cake, ice cream, chips and dip. Also, there was fruit punch. Tobias kept his eyes on the fruit punch, in case someone tried to spike the punch. Surprisingly, he was happy to be there to attend at a normal High School event. Tobias knew his parents would be proud. Tammy notified Tobias, they better dance on the floor before another guy ask her. So, Tobias stood up from his chair and danced with Tammy.

The dance floor was crowded. People were dancing back to back with other couples. Then, other couples were conversing about school activities. Suddenly, 2 High School guys eased through the crowd of dancers on the floor. The 2 High School guys snuck by in a plastic bag, a bottle of clear liquor in concealment. Tobias observed them pouring the liquor in the punch. Therefore, he advised Tammy about the punch. Tammy informed him, it's our Prom night. She said, "It is only a little alcohol. Besides, students expect the punch to be spiked anyways". This was Prom tradition. Therefore, Tobias notified Melvin, which the punch was spiked. Melvin informed marvelous. Then, he retrieved him a cup to drink.

Unfortunately, everyone who Tobias informed about the punch being spiked, decided to rush and retrieve them a cup to drink. Pretty soon, school administration staff had an event center full of drunken High School students. Tobias realized he was one of the few who wasn't drunk or tipsy. Then, soon, there were students who decided to venture over to the after-Prom party at the motel. Tobias tried to inform students about staying abstinent from sex after the Prom. He handed out flyers to prevent teenage sex. Most students appeared unconcerned. Some students only laughed at his plea. Tammy even persuaded him to end the campaign during the event because she believed it was useless. Then, he noticed Tammy's eyes a little glossy. Tammy had been drinking also.

Tobias thought how he was going to be the Booty Guard, when everybody had been drinking. Now, people feel free to be promiscuous. When Tobias reached the motel, he escorted Tammy to the front entrance. Nostalgia sat outside and watched him with Tammy. She asked Tobias, "Could she have a word with him?" So, Tobias informed he was on a date; and he could only speak for a second. Tammy departed him and walked on the inside. Nostalgia informed he was taking a date to the motel; and it wasn't Helen. Didn't he know Helen cared for him. Tobias declared he knew now; but it was his duty to be his date's protector. Nostalgia notified him; this was not going to go smoothly. Then, Melvin arrived with his date and the rest of Tobias' friends.

The after-Prom party was a job for Tobias as the Booty Guard. Tobias did not rest the entire night. He stayed on high alert and found High School guys trying to influence their date to have sex in all different places. One couple was making out on a park bench; and Tobias separated them. Another couple was talking about having sex in the motel; and Tobias informed them; they must prevent teenage sex. Then, Tammy's had her hands all over Tobias. However, Tobias noticed Helen arrived and was monitoring the event. So, he informed Tammy; he would only entertain her for a little. Then, he would take her home. Suddenly, Mr. Johnson appeared. Melvin and Mr. Johnson tried to check out a motel room. Tobias notified the front desk. The motel made all their rooms occupied.

Therefore, when a High School student tried to check in a room to have sex, security announcements were made, which they had cameras to monitor the area. Also, the school department would receive a copy of the tape. Then, Tobias reported to the motel security of a man who was molesting teenage boys. Once Mr. Johnson heard security was looking for an adult who had a history of molesting teenagers, then Mr. Johnson departed the motel. Nevertheless, Tammy gave one more pitch for romance with Tobias. She confirmed with Tobias; they should take advantage of the opportunity to stay in a room because he works there. Furthermore, they should make the night memorial by sleeping together. Tobias reminded Tammy; he has sex phobias, which prevent him from sex.

At the end of the night, Tobias departed the motel, as Helen and Nostalgia watched. Tobias took Tammy home. He felt good about his accomplishments. Then, as Tobias arrived home, he called Helen to inform her about his safety. Helen was happy about his safe arrival home. Tobias informed her, no sex occurred between his date and him. Although, Helen notified she was not happy because she worried if he would have sex. Tobias informed he didn't know she was this jealous of him. Helen notified she cared for him; and if he ever wanted sex again, then he should be with her. Tobias was shocked. He became emotional and notified Helen, he cared for her also. Senior year in High School was ending; and Tobias began to feel, he needed to think more about his life after school.

The next school day at a Prevent teenage sex rally, Tobias realized the Seniors in High School were not happy with his booty guard duty. Because of Tobias, the Seniors blamed him for having a losing football team, boring Prom and boring school year. Tobias tried to sympathize with the students by informing them, a lot of good has happened. The Booty Guard had almost eliminated school teenage pregnancy. Also, it had kept sexual harassment and sexual assault down in High School. Before booty guard duty, there were little regulations in place to stop anyone from becoming a sex victim. Although, the times may had been strict on social life but overall, school life had improved. Then the students began booing Tobias. Mercedes tried to defend Tobias from the disruptive crowd.

It was no help. Mercedes realized despite what she had said or done, students hated Tobias and his booty guard duty. She consoled Tobias; then, informed the booty guard duties were not what the students wanted anymore. School Administrators reassured Tobias; his booty guard duty will be kept in place because it made the schools safer. Although, Tobias the Booty Guard held his head down in school because now, he was ashamed of his accomplishments. High School football players who preyed on their cheerleaders were upset because they believed Tobias ended their fun. They began to make plans to reassure their High School Football Convention would not be boring because of Tobias. Ricky notified the football team; he had an emergency plan to guarantee fun.

During the end of the school day, Tobias sat in his Dodge automobile and meditated. The feeling Tobias had was mixed up. Tobias first belief was sexual misconduct should be punished and prohibited everywhere. Who cares if the relationships were cordial with the misconduct? Although, Tobias realized sexual feelings between people who loved each other could be beautiful. Who don't want to show their feelings for love? Love was the International language all over the world. To show love in public was no crime. It was the way you show love, which caused problems. Tobias wondered, if being the Booty Guard was wrong. He had to confide with his mother, which he didn't want to do. He knew what his father would say already.

When Tobias arrived home from school, he put his things away. Ms. Elle was cleaning up in the kitchen and preparing to walk in the neighborhood for to visit a neighbor. Tobias hated his father would allow her to do this on a regular basics. So, he decided to walk with her until she reached her destination. Once they begin to walk, Ms. Elle knew Tobias had something on his mind, which was bothering him. Therefore, Ms. Elle inquired to Tobias, what was the matter. Tobias explained he didn't like her walking in the neighborhood alone. Although, Ms. Elle told him, she knew this already; but what else. Furthermore, Tobias told Ms. Elle, he felt depressed because people don't like him protecting individuals from sexual abuse.

Ms. Elle stopped walking and turned to face him. She wanted to know; what people would have problems with this. Tobias informed almost everyone. Ms. Elle notified him; one time, she was involved with helping women escape from sex trafficking during the early days of her life, before he was born. Mr. Rogers Nelson who worked at the airport, assisted the women with travel arrangements out of the area, while Ms. Elle drove the women to the airport. The women were staffed at the motel bar. Mr. Williams who was the Motel Manager worked in security at the time. Unfortunately, the Motel Manager who was working was allowing the sex trafficking to occur. Eventually, the Motel Manager got prosecuted and lost his job. Then, Mr. Williams became Motel Manager.

For this reason, Ms. Elle and Mr. Nelson were conscious of victims of sex abuse. They continued to monitor the news for victims of sex abuse because it once was their passion to prevent crimes of sex abuse. Although, over time Mr. Nelson became nonactive because of the dangers associated with helping victims. Ms. Elle albeit, still made rounds in the neighborhood to prevent crimes such as sex abuse. She walked through neighborhoods, while introducing herself to people and does her neighborhood watch routine. Then, she has discussions at home with Mr. Nelson about sex abuse. Apparently, Tobias must have learned something about sex abuse victims from Ms. Elle and Mr. Nelson's conversations because he is entirely sympathetic towards sex abuse.

When Tobias heard this, he felt rejuvenated. Tobias realized he wasn't crazy for his feelings to protect the weak, misinformed or naïve human being who underestimated the tragedies of becoming a sex victim. It became critical for Tobias to use all his strength, influence and power to stop all victims of sex crimes. Regardless, what people said or did, he was using his powers to stop the sex abuse. He thought his first mission would be to stop Mr. Johnson the football coach and his sexual advances on teenagers. Mr. Johnson had been getting away too long. He was coaching at Jr. High School and then, he got promoted to High School. This was the main reason; why he didn't play football. It wasn't because he was too busy working as the Booty Guard or motel. That was only an excuse.

Therefore, Tobias made plans to stop Mr. Johnson's escapades. Then, next he would continue to promote his prevent teenage sex rallies and persuade Mercedes to keep up the fight. However, the negativity from High School students about the Booty Guard would need to stop. Tobias' close friends like Melvin, Ricky, Sherri, Persia, Tammy, Tracy, Craig and anyone else who wanted to ridicule his passion to protect the needed, they would need to abolish their doubts because the Booty Guard was him. Tobias realized he wasn't going to change, until sex crimes were wiped away from North City Town H.S for good. When he returned to school, he was motivated. In addition, he couldn't wait to return for work.

Ricky booked Motel rooms with Mr. Johnson's assistance for all the football players. Motel front desk had no clue with ideas which were being planned. Although, Mr. Williams accommodated booked Motel rooms. The motel had an understanding about the Football Convention; but no one knew, what all the Motel rooms were booked for. Peradventure, Mr. Johnson claimed it was for an appreciation for his football players because they worked hard as a team. Therefore, they deserved a night of luxury and fun. Then, Sherri negotiated a night of sex and passion with female workers to entertain the football players. Sherri had been noticing the flyers which had solicited female sex and a night of pleasure with a monetary fee. She took the flyers to Ricky because he wanted sexual pleasure for his football teammates.

When Tobias arrived for work, Nostalgia was sitting on a park bench as normal. Nostalgia was dressed in casual wear, a sweater and jeans. Tobias approached her with kindness. He informed her, she was dressed in casual wear, which was appropriate for him. So, Nostalgia informed Tobias; he be so concerned about her attire and not concerned enough for her daughters' wear. Helen looked nice too; and she is interested in him. Nostalgia couldn't understand, why Tobias didn't like Helen as well. Tobias informed he did like Helen; even-though, they had differences in opinions. Therefore, Nostalgia told Tobias; Helen wants a man who will take charge and satisfy her in the bedroom. Nostalgia explained, if Tobias would escort her somewhere quiet like a Motel room.

Tobias informed Nostalgia, he was told not to allow her inside the motel. Nostalgia notified Tobias; she was part owner of the motel. She had the rights to be sleeping in a Motel room whenever she wanted too. Tobias notified her; Helen told me, you are part Motel owner and her mother. So, this is true? Nostalgia looked with wide eyes in amazement. She informed Tobias, show me a Motel room; and she will explain something to him. Tobias escorted Nostalgia to a Motel room. He grabbed a set of Motel keys from the front desk before arriving to a room. As the Motel room door opened, Nostalgia walked inside, shoved Tobias inside the room and closed the door. Nostalgia looked at him in the eyes and said, "For you to satisfy my daughter, she needed to see what he was working with".

Therefore, Tobias had to satisfy Nostalgia sexually. Tobias informed Nostalgia, clarify herself because he was not having sex with her. Nostalgia notified Tobias, he must pretend she was Helen and do to her, whatever he thought Helen would enjoy sexually. Tobias thought and closed his eyes. Nostalgia undressed her clothes and Tobias grimace. He declared he was unprepared. So, Nostalgia informed she was prepared. Nostalgia's opened her pocketbook. Tobias informed he would kiss her all over her body. Nostalgia took dental wrap protection from her pocketbook. Then, she grabbed a condom out. Tobias gave a low screamed from surprise. He quietly began undressing his clothes. Then, Nostalgia began to smile.

Time passed and Helen looked for Tobias. Mr. Williams were looking for Tobias. Therefore, Mr. Williams and Helen searched through hallways looking for Tobias. They requested for Tobias to check in by radio because Tobias carried a handheld radio. Helen walked down the Motel hallway and noticed Nostalgia coming out a Motel room. Then, she noticed Tobias coming out the Motel room fixing his clothes on his body. Helen approached Nostalgia quickly and said, "Mama how could you!" Helen looked in shock and informed she was only testing out the Booty Guard's stamina. Nevertheless, a person cannot be a good Booty Guard, unless he has a taste of what he's protecting. Now, he knows the reasons to be a Booty Guard.

However, Tobias tried to explain to Helen; he was tricked by Nostalgia to perform sex because he wanted to be sexually experienced for her. Helen became so angry with Nostalgia and Tobias. Although, she knew her mother was cunning, when it came to sex. Therefore, Helen forgave Tobias; but he had to promise, he would be faithful to her for now on. Tobias made the promise; but he wouldn't trust Nostalgia anymore. Nostalgia apologized. She informed to Tobias; he needs to stop being concerned about her needs because she was deprived from sex by Helen and now with him performing the Booty Guard. Mr. Williams and Nostalgia were divorced. Furthermore, Nostalgia believed she had to move on with her life sexually. Even-though, Nostalgia wanted Helen to be satisfied with a man sexually.

Mr. Williams feelings for Nostalgia and Tobias' sexual encounter, was Helen's concern for Tobias. He promised Tobias, he would see about his best interest. Albeit, Tobias would have to be in good standings with his daughter and him. Mr. Williams cared less about Nostalgia's sexual escapades because he couldn't fill her needs anyway. It became a loss, which he had to partner with his ex-wife or lose the motel. Although, it benefited him dearly to keep the motel because he wanted to establish economic stability for his family. Also, Tobias the Booty Guard really had been an asset because he was one of the best in security. Previously, there had been problems with female staff at the Motel bar. Tobias and his fear of sexual assaults have almost eliminated all incidents.

It had come to time for the Football Convention. Mr. Williams would normally be the host. Albeit, Motel crimes had drastically, went down. Therefore, Mr. Williams believed he could delegate his duties to someone else. The City Mayor wanted to meet about the City Galilee at a nearby restaurant. So, Mr. Williams decided to meet with the Mayor. It had come to Mr. Williams attention, he wanted to leave Nostalgia with Motel responsibilities occasionally because it appeared, she did nothing at all but make appointments to sleep with clients. When Mr. Williams informed Nostalgia, she would be in-charge of the Football Convention, she was more than happy.

During the day, Nostalgia informed staff members, she would be in-charge. Although, Tobias was in school. A phone call was made about rooms being booked and female staff performing sexual duties. Nostalgia was extremely overjoyed. She realized her flyers were working by permission of Mr. Williams. To boost business, Mr. Williams informed Nostalgia to do something. Therefore, she did what she knew best, which was start a prostitution service for Motel guest.

CHAPTER 4

Accountability Report

IT WAS HER MISSION TO have a business on the side because she was tired of partnering with Mr. Williams. In addition, the flyers created additional Motel customers. The proof was the rooms being booked for the Football Convention. Nostalgia's only concern was the Booty Guard. Therefore, she notified her long-time friend Police Chief Mr. Whitehouse, in-case of any incidents.

Football players were excited at North City Town H.S. Ricky and Persia made plans to finally get revenge on Tobias. Then, Mr. Johnson, the football coach was involved also. They didn't like Tobias ruining their High School experience. It was the feeling, which they felt no control of their school experience because Tobias had created this school atmosphere. The school atmosphere where the School administration was paranoid of teenage sexual prowess. It was harmless and insignificant to them, how Tobias acted as if the Booty Guard was needed. Besides, the football players believed he was only trying to establish publicity for himself because they heard he wanted to work in a career with the Police Department.

Ricky became intimidated with Tobias and the booty guard service. Although, Tobias was his friend. Then again, a Booty Guard to Ricky and his girlfriend. Ricky didn't like the service. He only accepted the service because of his girlfriend Sherri. If it wasn't for the fact, which Tobias was a big guy, then Ricky would give him a beat down. Persia couldn't control Tobias; so, Ricky wouldn't attempt to control Tobias either, especially, on a solo basics. Perhaps, as a football team together, they could give Ricky the revenge he needed. It was a tragedy to Ricky, which Tobias acquired a sex phobia from his sexual encounter with Mr. Johnson. Albeit, this was the ammunition the football team needed to get revenge on Tobias. Therefore, Ricky requested to book as many rooms possible at the motel for freaky sexual encounters.

From the school administration, staff and parents, North City Town H.S became a model institution, which changed from a lack of interest to a school discipline to be praised and worshiped. The school on the inside was cleaned spotless every night; and the outside area was maintained down to the cracks in the parking lots. Furthermore, the students and teachers were trained to operate on their best behavior. Tobias entered the school building and clearly, it was a totally different school from his Freshman to Senior year. He noticed certain students performing as Booty Guards, which was his designated assistants. It made him proud, which the school administration found the booty guard service important. Although, clearly, everyone did not have the same feeling.

As Tobias walked pass the break area, there were football players discussing about the Booty Guard. They were making plans as if there weren't going to be anymore booty guard rules. Some football players were making plans for establishing social parties and saluting farewell to Tobias the Booty Guard. Tobias wondered what this greeting was about. The Booty Guard was not going nowhere. It was a thriving and pertinent position at North City Town H.S. A High School girl escorted by a Booty Guard assistant claimed football players were going to petition against the Booty Guards in school. Furthermore, Tobias was going to lose his reputation as someone who cared about sexual assaults. Worry showed on Tobias face because football players were plotting against him.

Therefore, Mercedes informed Tobias; there was always someone available who needed the booty guard service. Peradventure, North City Town H.S might not be proper for your ideas. Then, you must take the Booty Guard to somewhere who do appreciate your service. Mercedes knew girls from a different High School who wished they had a booty guard service to escort them inside shopping malls. Tobias thought about the idea. Then, he informed Mercedes; it is sad, I didn't think about other areas which needed the Booty Guard too. Tobias realized he couldn't keep the Booty Guard for only at school. He had to do it at work and everywhere he went. The Booty Guard was supposed to go, where anyone was in distress.

After school, Tobias departed to his home. Tammy was sitting on his doorstep. Tobias thought about her unhappiness with the Booty Guard. He greeted Tammy, politely saying hello, can I help you. Tammy informed Tobias, she was sorry, which she thought the booty guard service needed to end. She wanted Tobias and not the booty guard service because it took away his time. Nevertheless, she informed him; she didn't care anymore about her classmates who were against the Booty Guard because they were mean and thoughtless. Tammy informed she cared about him. Tobias smiled in satisfaction; but he told Tammy, he couldn't be with her. He notified his love was for Helen; and he had to get ready to work at the Football Convention. Tammy became sad and departed.

Ms. Elle and Mr. Rogers Nelson observed Tammy walking away from the doorsteps disgruntled with Tobias. So, they wondered the reasons why she was upset. Tobias notified his parents; Tammy doesn't understand the Booty Guard. Ms. Elle informed the Booty Guard was only a job. Although, Tobias was a real person. One day, Tobias will get tired and old like his daddy. The sex phobias would have gone away. It will come a time, where he will want a person who appreciates Tobias and not the Booty Guard. Tobias informed his mother; he was the Booty Guard and nobody would change this. Then, Mr. Nelson notified Tobias; if he was hosting the Football Convention, then he better gets moving because traffic was going to be heavy.

Tobias left in his Dodge Charger and the traffic was heavy. There were vehicles struggling to find decent parking spaces to attend the Football Convention. Therefore, Tobias parked his vehicle in the security parking space. Then, he got out his vehicle and helped to direct traffic at the Convention Center. The school activity bus which North City Town H.S used for travel, arrived; and football players exited the bus. It was obvious, Mr. Johnson and Ricky were leading the football players because they were having private discussions for a few minutes. Afterwards, they brief the athletes on the outside and entered the Convention area. Spectators with Tobias observed the activities of the football players, while fans clapped with happiness as they marched inside the building.

The Convention Center was decorated to show artifacts of the great Football Legends who attended North City Town H.S. As the players entered, they passed all the artifacts and became emotional. Tobias followed behind as he escorted a few High School cheerleaders on the inside. Melvin was part of the cheerleading staff. He informed Tobias; we don't need your service anymore because the Booty Guard was not wanted. A shocked look appeared on Tobias face. Tobias informed the cheerleaders; he was only trying to help. Then, the football players names were being announced to obtain their reward for their service. Tobias stood by the exit door. Mr. Johnson made the final announcement and the ceremony ended.

By the time the ceremony ended, Tobias rushed to assist the security staff with the heavy traffic. It had become late, dark and dangerous for anyone to be wandering around. As Tobias waited until the last vehicle departed, a security personnel informed him; his service was needed at the motel. However, Tobias notified he only had a little time left on his shift. Although, he would do what he can to help. Tobias drove by the bar and it was completely closed. So, he thought this was good. Then, he made a security walk inside the motel. It was like a convention inside the lobby. Front desk was in chaos. The desk clerk told football players were disturbing the first floor. Football players were spotted here and there. They were everywhere, where a disturbance was happening.

Tobias informed he should call Mr. Williams. The front desk clerk implied; Mr. Williams was not available. He left Ms. Nostalgia Williams in charge of the Motel for the night. Nevertheless, Tobias didn't trust Nostalgia; so, he called Helen. No reply came over the radio. Therefore, Tobias walked on every floor in the motel. Surprisingly, female workers were parading in lingerie attire and walking loosely on the upper motel floors. It was as if football players had gone sex wild because they were hugging, groping and kissing the female workers. Some female workers were screaming for help and calling security. It was Tobias' worst nightmare because there was hardly enough security for assistance. Somebody informed Tobias to notify police.

A call was notified to police by Tobias. Unfortunately, the phone operator informed, the wait time for assistance was 15 minutes. Then, a football player who Tobias recognized, told of Persia was assaulting a female staff. A feeling of disbelief touched Tobias. Tobias thought about Persia having a set back with his therapy. He figured Persia wasn't supposed to be getting into any more trouble and sexual assaulting another female. So, he ran to find Persia. It became a race against time because sexual assault happens fast. Tobias began running down a motel floor, which supposedly Persia's room was located. Then, he heard a voice from a room. It wasn't Persia's voice who he heard. It was Melvin's voice. Then, he heard Mr. Johnson's voice.

Melvin was crying and pleading for mercy. It appeared as Mr. Johnson was assaulting Melvin. The sound of a wounded dog sounded better to Tobias. Therefore, Tobias knocked on the door. They didn't stop. Heavy breathing was heard and more crying. Mr. Johnson notified Tobias; you can't help Melvin now. Go help someone else. Tobias shouted no! Look Mr. Johnson, we can discuss this. Although, Mr. Johnson only laughed. Persia opened his room door and laughed. He informed Tobias, it's too late. Go do something else because you are a bad Booty Guard. The women here are ours. We paid for this service and the Booty Guard can't stop a thing! Panic hit Tobias. He couldn't breathe. The thought of everyone there sexually involved with an affair. It was too much. Tobias had a panic attack.

No one came to Tobias assistance. Mr. Williams and Helen were not there. The police response was slow. Melvin became a victim of sexual assault. Motel security gave Tobias very little assistance. They eventually, escorted Tobias away because of shock. The stress which Tobias took was too great. Paramedics serviced Tobias and brought him back to stable condition. The police and Mr. Williams felt sad over the incident. Although, Mr. Williams recognized Tobias' dedication to victims of sexual assault, abuse and harassment. A week of vacation was given to Tobias for recovery of stress. This made Tobias have a different attitude. Then, school graduation was coming up; and Tobias wasn't sure where his life was going to go. It was time for Tobias to make decisions about his life.

Tobias woke up in bed worried. His first thought was Melvin and the Motel female staff. He picked up the phone and decided to call the motel. The front desk reported no serious crimes in the blog but there were complaints of loud noise disturbances in the motel. Flashbacks of the Motel incidents slowly came to Tobias, as he tried to get his thoughts together. It was a nightmare for Tobias because he couldn't control the safety of people he knew. Untamed sex had run rampant in the Motel rooms, while Tobias was short of assistance. Football players who were his associates in school treated him as the enemy, while they indulged in their sexual desires. Tobias concluded, if they wanted to throw their lives away on reckless sex, then he had to use drastic measures to control their ambitions.

Therefore, Tobias needed to verify Melvin's condition. Melvin's phone rang, when Tobias called him. The call went straight to voicemail. Tobias pleaded on Melvin's voicemail for him to answer the phone. He needed conformation, which Melvin was okay. Then, Tobias called another number. Ms. Dundry answered the phone and she was highly upset. Ms. Dundry informed to Tobias; Melvin doesn't want to talk on the phone now. This was very different for Melvin because he loved to talk with anybody on the phone. Ms. Dundry knew this; so, she expected something was wrong with Melvin. Tobias notified Ms. Dundry; he apologized for Melvin's condition. Then, Ms. Dundry inquired to Tobias, what condition. Suddenly, Melvin answered the phone.

Melvin told Tobias; he shouldn't tell, he had a condition. He was only embarrassed of the Motel incident and sad. Melvin acknowledge he was stubborn and should have listen to Tobias. He wished he was more careful around Mr. Johnson because he turned something which was supposed to have been beautiful into something bad. Tobias informed Melvin; he regretted not being able to prevent what happened to him. He was Melvin's Booty Guard and he failed him. Melvin notified Tobias; he wasn't upset because he thought it was love. When you feel love, you take risk, which is life. Melvin was grateful to be experiencing life. He informed Tobias; he wasn't ashamed to have lost love with a man or anyone. Furthermore, Tobias ought to make at least one effort for love.

It was tragedy, what Melvin recalled to Tobias. Mr. Johnson putting his hands around his neck and choking him. Then, he took a pocket knife out his pocket and held it to Melvin's side. Mr. Johnson who was a slender built man, was stronger and quicker than Melvin. Tobias knocked on the door and requested for Melvin to speak. Although, he only heard heavy breathing. Unfortunately, Melvin could not speak because Mr. Johnson had a choke hold on Melvin's neck. Therefore, Melvin breathed extremely heavy before he made screams of terror. However, Mr. Johnson planned for it to be a terrible scene. Mr. Johnson wanted it to sound, as if he was raping and killing Melvin, which would disturb Tobias tremendously. When Tobias pleaded with Mr. Johnson to stop, Mr. Johnson realized he had accomplished his mission. Therefore, he just laughed in pleasure.

After Melvin told Tobias his story about the incident, Tobias cried in sadness. Melvin comfort Tobias, by hugging him and kissing him on his forehead. Then, Melvin informed Tobias; he was the best Booty Guard and friend in the world. Tobias informed Melvin; criminal charges should be made to Mr. Johnson and the football team. Melvin had forbidding any criminal prosecution to anyone. Therefore, Tobias planned a revenge by another way. School graduation was coming fast. So, Tobias figured something had to be done soon before they graduated. Nevertheless, while Tobias was out of work for a week, he thought of a plan. Once he returned to school, School administration had ended the booty guard assistance because of Tobias failures to stop chaos in the Motel. Then, North City Town H.S returned to past routines.

Tobias returned with a vengeance. He notified football players, how wrong it was for them to be fornicating and creating chaos at the W-S Prime Motel. Furthermore, it was a lack of respect for him, they did this at his job. However, Tobias believed they did this because they were angry with him being the Booty Guard. Therefore, Tobias determined he should take his services somewhere else. Other students, from other areas have requested the booty guard service. So, now, Tobias has considered to work for them. Mercedes was overjoyed to find Tobias helping students, who appreciate him better. Also, the Booty Guard was in big demand to escort women in shopping malls and fancy club gatherings.

Although, the extra booty guard work did not deviate Tobias from his main priorities. Tobias kept his eyes on sexual assault occurrences at his school and motel. He also studied hard to receive his H.S diploma during graduation. Then, he kept his plan secret for revenge of Mr. Johnson and the football players. Surprisingly, Mr. Williams notified Tobias; a referral was done by him to attend Police Academy after his graduation from High School. It was Tobias dreams to work for the Victims Unit with the Police Department. All Tobias had to do now, was keep up the good work at the motel and do a good security job for the City Galilee. The City Galilee was most important because Mr. Williams had personal relationships with the City Police Chief and Mayor of Winston-Salem.

Mr. Williams informed Tobias; the City Police Chief was a meticulous man and one not to waste time with. The Police Chief was short and stout. He had gray streaks in his hair and laugh distinctly. Whenever the City Police Chief would arrive at the motel, Mr. Williams would escort him; and it would be for only brief moments. Although, Helen despised the Police Chief. Helen informed Tobias; he was corrupt and used his powers to obtain special favors. She would request Tobias to give her booty guard service, whenever she heard the Police Chief was in the motel. Although, this didn't bother Tobias because he was catching feelings for Helen. Therefore, it became difficult for Tobias to have a good relationship with the Police Chief.

During the City Galilee, Tobias believed every important City leader was there. Tobias had to put on his best behavior. Mr. Williams had guaranteed in a safety briefing, he would receive his career dream, if he could impress the City Galilee guest. So, Tobias did his best to make sure everyone was safe. At the front desk of the motel, Tobias noticed private rooms had been booked inside the motel. Last time, Tobias notice a lot of private rooms being booked, it was at the Football Convention. A little anxiety was felt by Tobias because private rooms meant less security and monitoring. However, it was mostly high-level city employees. Then, the front desk announced a message was left for Tobias. So, Tobias read the message.

It was Helen requesting him to escort her from the bar to the motel because the City Galilee party was finished. Tobias felt a sense to be a little concern because he figured the Police Chief might be in the area. Therefore, when he departed the motel and arrived at the bar, he heard Helen was gone. Nostalgia notified she left with the Police Chief. She laughed and told him his actions better be fast. Tobias didn't understand and Nostalgia wouldn't explain her reasons for telling his this. Although, he noticed a lot of female staff were missing. As Tobias returned to the main lobby of the motel, the front desk informed him; female escort workers were in the motel. Flyers were passed out, soliciting female sex for hire. It was Tobias worst nightmare.

The female sex workers had on uniforms, which looked like maid service; except, they wore fish net stockings and high heel shoes. They carried themselves professional, but they were seductive. Some women's attire had low cleavage, which exposed their breast enough to draw men's attention. Then, other sex workers swayed as they walked to draw men's attention. Although, most of the sex workers were already obligated to their clients and didn't draw attention at all. The sex workers only waited patiently in the Motel lobby, for to meet a City worker on a rendezvous. Tobias would had thought the sex workers were late night maid service, until identified by front desk. So, now, he recognized their routine, when they operated for business.

Tobias notified Mr. Williams to call the police. Mr. Williams called the police and informed Tobias to stay calm, while guarding the front desk. Tobias began to panic; and Mr. Williams reminded him to stay calm and don't allow the female escort workers to make him upset. So, Tobias followed instructions and returned to the front desk. Once Tobias arrived at the front desk, he remembered to notify Mr. Williams about his daughter being missing. Mr. Williams told Tobias; Helen wasn't missing because she is in the motel with the Police Chief. Tobias panicked and told Mr. Williams, he felt as if his daughter was in trouble. Therefore, Mr. Williams with Nostalgia met Tobias and explain to him at the front desk. Simultaneously, Nostalgia was passing out the flyers soliciting female prostitution. Tobias looked with his mouth open and eyes wide.

Mr. Williams asked Tobias, "What was his problem?" Nostalgia was performing a duty. Tobias became upset and told Mr. Williams, this was not a good thing, they were doing. Mr. Williams informed Tobias, if he was having another panic attack, then he could call 911. Albeit, if he wasn't, then he should continue working as if everything was normal. Tobias could not believe Mr. Williams told him this. It destroyed his joy. Tobias realized Mr. Williams and Nostalgia were having prostitution in their motel and it was terrible. Tobias loved his job; but he couldn't handle women selling themselves for Mr. Williams' profits. Nostalgia was right because Mr. Williams knew what was happening all alone. Tobias' father was right because Mr. Williams was corrupted.

Nevertheless, Nostalgia had sexual relations with Tobias because she wanted to change his opinion on sex. Nostalgia hated Tobias had a sex phobia. Mr. Williams and Nostalgia tried to explain to Tobias, it was only sex; and the female staff were performing their duties as workers. Nevertheless, Helen was with the Police Chief conducting an important business meeting in her office, which was a Motel room full of sex gadgets. Tobias was told, the sex gadgets were for him because he had been with a man. Peradventure, he thought the sex with Nostalgia was for his experience. Although, it wasn't for him but for them. Tobias even wondered, did Helen really cared about him; or she was just toying with his emotions. He wanted to leave and talk to someone.

The Booty Guard, who Tobias thought was important, now had lost his confidence and will to survive. He wondered what to do. Tobias made himself think proactively. He told Mr. Williams; he had things to do before going home because his shift was ending. Mr. Williams notified Tobias, for him to do what he needed before leaving and get himself together with his phobias. So, Tobias departed from Mr. Williams. He slowly, walked to Mr. Williams office. Tobias took a blank disc and made copies of all the monitoring tapes of Mr. Johnson and the football team. Then, he made copies of the female escort workers. As Tobias departed Mr. Williams office, he barely escaped from being detected by Nostalgia. Fortunately for Tobias, Nostalgia didn't ask him any questions.

Therefore, Tobias rushed from the motel because he had to talk with someone else about his problems. What decision to make, Tobias didn't know at first. So, Tobias called his older brother Reggie to discuss his problems. Reggie told Tobias, to meet him at the Red Roof Lounge. It was a place from the other side of the District area. The Red Roof Lounge advertised as a hangout for the young working adults. Most of the customers were from age 20 to 35. The roof of the building was red and the outside resembled a barn. The music played was Urban house beat music, which could be heard from outside. On the inside, chandeliers hung from the sky and a bar sat about 12 feet long. Waiter staff walked everywhere inside the building serving beer and mixed drinks.

Once Tobias and Reggie met there, then they began to talk freely. Reggie informed Tobias, forget about your problems, the tapes and Booty Guard service. What you need, is a night of fun. Once again, Reggie tried to persuade Tobias into having a sexual encounter. Reggie negotiated with female club workers to socialize with Tobias. Therefore, female workers brought Tobias a drink to be friendly. At first Tobias wanted to refuse but he was depressed. So, he began to drink to forget about his problems.

A girl named Gloria, who was a waitress listened to Tobias aspirations of healing the world from sex criminals. Gloria informed Tobias, what was he, a superhero or something because she never met a person with such a compassion for sex victims?

After Tobias drank more, he informed Gloria; no one really appreciated the Booty Guard. Tobias told he had done booty guard service for his High School, job and friends; yet, no one loves him. Gloria showed sympathy and concern, which made Tobias happy. Tobias informed Reggie, the Booty Guard only wants peace. The Booty Guard stands for love and happiness, not hate. He wasn't trying to be a love blocker. The Booty Guard only wants to be a street rocker. The women at the bar table laughed. Then, Reggie asked Gloria, "Would she take care of Tobias and show him a good time because he wasn't ready to go home?" The female staff lady informed Reggie, sure she would because Tobias was her type of man. As Reggie departed the lounge alone, unfortunately Tobias commenced to drink more and began to act differently. Tobias personality became too friendly.

Tobias began kissing everyone in the lounge. He kept repeating, he loved each and everyone. Therefore, Tobias thought he had to prove, how the Booty Guard could be a loving person too. So, whenever Tobias observed someone in the club, he kissed them passionately. Sadly, Tobias kissed an unfriendly person; and she complained to the bar attendant. Therefore, the bar attendant announced for security. Tobias arrived informing he could give someone assistance. The bar attendant informed he can assist escorting himself out the club because he was the problem. Therefore, Gloria exited out the bar behind Tobias. Tobias notified he once again was a failure. Gloria promised Tobias, his problems will eventually, work themselves out because he was a great guy.

Gloria chaperone Tobias to his car. They sat inside the car; and Tobias began sobbing. Tobias informed he just wanted to be loved and appreciated. Gloria kissed him and informed he was a stranger but she loved him. They kissed more and it began to become passionate. Then, Tobias thought and stopped kissing. Suddenly, Tobias began to sob again. The woman asked Tobias, "What was wrong because she could try and make it better?" Tobias informed her; he needed to be at home because his mind wasn't in a good place. Therefore, Tobias took Gloria to a designate place and drove away. It was early Saturday morning, so Tobias drove around the District area. He passed the motel and realized the Police Chief stayed in the motel overnight. So, Tobias slept the rest of the morning in his automobile.

When Tobias awaken, there were female sex workers leaving the motel. Then, Tobias found the Police Chief leaving, after a passionate kiss on Helen's cheek. Tobias drove a scratch mark in the Motel parking lot. Motel staff recognized Tobias. They became shocked because Tobias appeared upset. Therefore, Tobias drove, while meditating about his life and career. Tobias reached the mall. School student girls recognized Tobias and requested him to be their escort in the mall. Tobias escorted the student girls inside the mall. Although, he was sad. Then, a homeless elderly man began making obscene gestures at the girls. So, Tobias told the man; he better calmed down before the Police Cops started looking for him.

The schoolgirls notified the homeless man; the Booty Guard was here to protect them from all sexual harassment, assault and rape. Parents who were in attendance watched as the Booty Guard pushed the homeless man down on the ground as he tried to approach the schoolgirls. The parents began clapping in enjoyment. They asked the Booty Guard, "What was his inspiration?" Then, Tobias informed he had a fear for all, who was involved in an unwanted sexual incident like rape, harassment or abuse. Tobias notified his main goal was to prevent all sex crimes and protect an individual's booty. A person's sex organs were an individual's ownership and no one else. So, happened news reporters located in the mall praised Tobias for a good job. Then, Tobias felt better about himself.

As Tobias woke up the next Sunday morning, he decided to attend church. The pastor of the church recognized Tobias was a little gloomy because he sat quiet alone. Therefore, he asked Tobias, "Was everything okay?" Tobias told the pastor; he had been feeling abnormal because he had gotten drunk in the nightclub and showed anger at work. Then, the pastor implied to Tobias; this was not his problem. Although, this was not good; but there was something more serious on his mind. Tobias did not speak. Therefore, the pastor said to Tobias, "Be, do, know. Be who you are. Do what you are known to do. Also, know what you can understand. Then, act on good behalf". At the end, Tobias found a better understanding of himself.

It was a conformation from God, what Tobias needed. Tobias had been feeling unsure of himself. He went home and told his parents; he had copies of disc tapes on City employees trying to bargain for sex. Then, he had classmates negotiating for sex in the Motel rooms. Last, he had his football coach in a Motel room with a minor, having sex; and it was all on disc tape. Mr. Rogers Nelson notified Tobias, what was his motivation for obtaining this information. Tobias notified he was quitting the Motel Security job. The disc tapes were for his reassurance, which Mr. Williams promised a good recommendation for the Police force. Tobias figured Mr. Williams wasn't going to allow him to quit and give him a good reference too, unless he used blackmail as a tool. Mr. Nelson was a little disappointed he didn't come to him sooner. Therefore, he made a phone call to the City Mayor about Tobias' problem.

Time had come for Tobias graduation. Tobias notified Mr. Williams; he wasn't working for him anymore because of the sex scandals in the motel. Although, he had proof, the sex scandals were real. So, Mr. Williams informed him; Mr. Whitehouse who was the Police Chief, wanted to give him an interview for a Police Officer job. Tobias was extremely happy. It appeared his dreams was coming to reality. Although, Tobias wasn't missing much work money because he was escorting students around in the mall and at social gatherings. Nevertheless, Tobias kept a few clients at his school, despite the football team's wishes. Therefore, High School graduation turned out to be a little different because things didn't go as students planned.

A line was formed at the Winston-Salem Auditorium for High School students' graduation. Tobias filled the line with students. He knew his family would be attending; so, he remained on his best behavior. When they called his name, the crowd had mixed emotions; but clearly, he heard his parents scream Tobias, while other students shouted the Booty Guard or just gave boos. Although, Tobias knew why he got the boos. Tobias was ridicule by the Football players. By then, Tobias stopped caring about the Football players displeasures. Perhaps, they became more upset, when a news reporter representing the T.V station gave him a personal close caption with an article mentioning the Booty Guard Celebrity. Then, Booty Guard haters turned a different tune.

Therefore, the Booty Guard boos became hurrahs! Albeit, they wanted camera shots for a chance to be on T.V too. Unfortunately, the camera man notified there wasn't enough time for everyone to be captured on camera. Then, Tobias got recognized by the City Mayor for reducing the city's crime rate on sex offenders. Also, Tobias was recognized by North City Town H.S for improving his school in sex violations and assistance in preventing sexual assaults in his neighborhood. Tobias had a list of participating stores at the mall, who congratulated him for preventing sex crimes inside the mall. Then, his Dad and Mom touched his sole by confession, they were proud to have him as their son. It almost appeared; the graduation had a special ceremony in care of Tobias. Then, there were others and their announcement.

The Auditorium was a facility which had historical events. Over time, the building had been remodeled and upgraded to standard art. It was a beautiful place located in the central area of North City Town H.S. Seating inside the Auditorium were luxurious and comfortable. Once seated, an individual believed they were inside a real amphitheater. Therefore, teachers and staff administrators knew it was a joy to host any event inside the Auditorium. So, student volunteers issued handouts which informed guest of the heritage of the Auditorium. Furthermore, there was a sense of a euphoria happening, which history was going to be made again in the Auditorium. Nevertheless, the audience stood on their feet to see the announcements.

Mr. Johnson figured he was going to announce a career move to Wake Forrest University. Although, plans backfired after Tobias sent disc copies of Mr. Johnson and Melvin checking into a Motel room to the Campus of Wake Forrest University. During a follow up meeting, Wake Forrest passed the disc tapes on to the Board of National Collegiate Administration Association. So, furthermore, Mr. Williams coaching career in NCAA was done, before it even begun. Nevertheless, Melvin ended up with a career in fashion clothes after graduating. Mercedes became a social media specialist. Ricky acquired Tobias' job as Motel Security Officer. Sherri continued to work for Helen as a Customer Service Worker. Persia became a College Football player. Tammy became a Banking Agent. Tracy and Craig became Community Social workers. Albeit, Mr. Johnson went to jail.

Therefore, after High School graduation, Tobias went home and prepared for an interview with the Police Chief. Tobias passed the interview. Although, he had to go through a process, before he entered the Police Academy. There were tests, Tobias had to take. First, Tobias took a physical test. While during the physical test, Tobias had to run 1 and a half miles, carrying a 150lb mannequin within 18 minutes. Then, next, he did 50 pushups and 50 sit ups, which was considered satisfactory. The next day, the City Police station checked his criminal record and he passed. Unfortunately, a negative report occurred on his psychological test. The person who administered the test failed him on the account of his moral judgement on sexual offenders. They asked him, "Do he believe there was a place for sexual offenders to be rehabilitated?"

CHAPTER 5

Jail crimes

TOBIAS ANNOTATED ON HIS TEST; he denied to answering the question. The psychiatrist informed Tobias, until he answered the question on the test, then his test was invalid and he failed. Tobias refused to answer because deep down inside his sole, a sex offender couldn't be trusted or rehabilitated. He became sadden how he felt and because he flunked the test. The psychiatrist referred him to another law enforcement branch, which was the Prison system. She notified to Tobias; the Prison system was where criminals got rehabilitated through corrections. Therefore, the Prison System would offer him a job as a Correction Officer. Then, it would show him how prisoners became corrected through time and training. Tobias was not happy. It wasn't what he really wanted. Although, he had to settle for this.

However, Tobias praised the Psychologist for finding a job for him. The Psychologist was married. So, Tobias believed he owed the Psychologist gratitude and could help her with booty guard service. He informed her, he was going to give her booty guard protection from sex predators, if he encounters her presence again because she was married. Although, the Psychologist denied the help. The Psychologist believed she was strong and could take care of herself, if a sex predator was harassing her. The Psychologist was beautiful and smart. Her name was Pamela and she caught Tobias eye. Pamela was strong; but she showed compassion. Tobias loved her compassion and believed Pamela was a good woman. So, he made a mental note to check on Pamela's safety when possible.

Winston Salem Prison system was a facility which housed convicts who were minimum, medium and close security. The different types of security were important to know because it depended on the crime they committed and how severe it was. Minimum security inmates were mostly bad check writers, con-artist and petty theft folks. Medium security were inmates who stole big items, molesters and trespassers. Close security were inmates who beat up people, threaten people or kill people. Tobias dealt with all three class of inmates. They gave him a tour on his first day of work of the entire facility. Once he got acquainted in his office, then he got introduced to the inmates assigned to his location.

The location for where Tobias was assigned, had 2 pods mixed with all classification of inmates. Although, they were mostly close. His supervisor was named Officer Bell. The Assistant Supervisor appeared to be nice because he made routine visit checks, unless the inmates were loose. This meant the inmates were roaming out of their rooms. Normally, they would be in the T.V room or out in the recreation yard, if they weren't lock down in their rooms. However, Tobias had the power to lock them in their rooms or unlock their room door and allow them to roam for fresh air. Although, when the inmates could roam, they were still confided to Tobias area because he had a locked gate surrounding his own area. Then, Tobias and Mr. Bell had the only access key to leave the area.

Tobias office had a desk and a comfortable chair; but Tobias mostly stood, so he could appear alert. Also, his office walls were made halfway to the top, out of bullet proof glass and halfway down out of bricks. Therefore, his office was bullet proof. From Tobias work office, over across the inmate recreation area was another office. It was the counselor's office. This office wasn't as safe because it did not have bullet proof windows. It only had a small window on the door. So, they would advise the counselor to leave the door open, when counseling an inmate. Unfortunately, inmates enjoyed entirely too much seeing counselors. This was one of the few moments, where the inmates could speak to someone on the outside of prison, besides speaking to a Correction Officer.

Mr. Bell would visit Tobias' office routinely to do accountability checks on Tobias's inmates and talk with him personally. He informed Tobias on a visit; he needed to make routine checks in the inmates living area to make sure they were safe. Also, he needed to escort inmates time to time outside his perimeter area, when they occur problems and needed to see administration. Although, Tobias should always keep his equipment on him, like handcuffs, baton and radio. Tobias main point of contact was his radio, but during emergencies he could use his telephone at his office desk. Therefore, Tobias didn't make calls on his phone much; but other security officers would call him, when they were bored. So, Tobias answered a phone call from another security officer named John.

John informed Tobias, he should communicate with his inmates less and not more because inmates only wanted to use him for evil deeds. He notified Tobias, the inmates were not his friend, no matter how friendly they appeared. Also, they could be dangerous, if they suspected he was weak mentally or physically. Therefore, he should contact them, only for their safety and to keep his job. So, Tobias was required to keep a daily logbook, which required him to annotate every hour, his safety checks of inmates' living areas. Nevertheless, it had become time for Tobias to make a safety check of his inmates. The first time Tobias walked alone in the inmate living areas, an inmate named Brown observed him and clapped his hands. The inmate was smiling.

Tobias asked Inmate Brown, "What are you so happy for?" Inmate Brown informed Tobias; he was happy because they finally have a Black Security Officer versus a Caucasian Security Officer. He told Tobias, Caucasian Security Officers are terrified of Black inmates and don't appear to care about their job. Therefore, Inmate Brown wanted Tobias to respond on his answer. Tobias informed Inmate Brown; he didn't experience any of this and believed all the Prison staff members cared about their job. Inmate Brown told Tobias; he believed Tobias cared about his job because he listens to inmates, when they have a problem. Although, another inmate named Julius looked at Tobias and didn't say a word. So, Tobias greeted him hello; and the inmate looked the other way in shame.

Next, Tobias finished making his safety check of all the inmates' living areas because he had 96 inmates assigned to him in 2 pods. As Tobias walked back to his office to lock both the inmate' pods, he heard somebody crying and moaning in agony. It wasn't a normal moan, but a moan which someone makes in a sexual encounter. The moan attracted Tobias attention because he had a fear of sexual assaults. Although,

Tobias couldn't pinpoint, where it was coming from. So, Tobias figured he needed a backup and radio called Mr. Bell. Tobias opened his gate for Mr. Bell. Then, Mr. Bell entered the gate and informed Tobias; he needed to lock the gate behind him.

After Tobias locked the gate, Mr. Bell and Tobias reentered the inmates' living area and heard an inmate crying. It was the inmate named Julius, who happened to be roommates with the inmate named Brown. So, Tobias and Bell escorted the Inmates' Brown and Julius out of their living areas unto the recreation yard to speak with them. Inmates' Brown and Julius declared everything was fine. Therefore, Mr. Bell sent them back to their living areas. Although, Tobias knew something strange was going on between the two inmates because Julius looked scared and Brown only smiled. Tobias realized it was a job for the Booty Guard. So, he had Julius sign a letter to be transferred to another living area.

Peradventure, Tobias felt good about himself because he thought he had done some good. The feeling of using his booty guard duties to protect someone made Tobias happy. Tobias felt the job of Corrections Officer suited him after all. Mr. Bell inquired how he was feeling about his job. Tobias informed he liked his job. Therefore, Mr. Bell sent him to a weeks' worth of Corrections Officer training, where Tobias learned more about his job. Tobias was happy, to be working somewhere to prevent sexual assaults. So, Tobias told his parents about his job. A thought appeared to Tobias, which he could be a family man like Mr. Bell with a career. Furthermore, Tobias went to church to praise God for all his blessings. Then, he noticed Tammy at his church.

While Tobias attended church to accept communion, Tammy was kneeling and praying. Therefore, he kneeled beside Tammy and prayed also. After praying, Tammy turned and looked at him. Tobias realized he made a mistake. He didn't know why he had overlooked Tammy. Perhaps because Tobias didn't know she attended church. Nevertheless, Tobias didn't know they had the same religion. Tammy informed she was visiting his church on a special occasion because they were affiliated. This was the reason, Ms. Elle and Tammy communicated. Tobias became amazed and observed Tammy a different way. He wondered, why his mother didn't tell him before this.

Tobias apologized to Tammy for not taking their relationship more serious because he was thinking about his career.

Then, Tobias informed he had a new job. Tobias informed he was training to learn how to be a Corrections Officer. Tammy informed she worked at the bank as a Bank Agent. Tobias thought it was great; she had a career job and went to college. Furthermore, they decided to spend time on a date. So, one day after training, Tobias picked Tammy up for a date. They decided to have dinner and attend church for a Bible Study group. It felt refreshing for Tobias, which he could learn about God with a girlfriend. It made Tobias feel different because they were in a Holy place of worship. Also, it was a rare time, which Tobias was on a date and he didn't have to think about the Booty Guard because they concentrated on praying.

Later, at the end of the date, Tobias took Tammy home. Tammy's mother smiled at Tobias. She was surprised to see him again. They begin to talk among each other and laughed about their family similarities because Tobias was a single child by his mother. Also, Tammy was too. Then, Tammy's mother called it a night because it had gotten late. Therefore, Tammy and Tobias were left alone in a dim light dining room. So, Tobias decided to say goodbye. Except, Tammy begin to say a prayer for Tobias' job and safety as they hold hands. Tobias became touched by the remarks. Next, he kissed Tammy on the lips. Then, told her thanks and good night. When he returned home, he called Tammy again. Suddenly, he asked Tammy, "Would she be his girlfriend?" Then, Tammy said, "Yes!"

It was a blessing for Tobias, which Tammy said, "Yes" because he wanted to have a family. After Tobias returned to work, his co-workers would meet in an employee lounge and have dinner. They would talk about their life away from work, their previous life and immediate family members. Most of the co-workers were married and had children. Tobias would be envious of the co-workers who had their own family and children. Although, Tobias was young, he looked forward to one day having his own family. The love, support and happiness, which one receives, when taking care of a family, Tobias wished to have this. Tammy and her family appeared to care for Tobias. Therefore, the Booty guard wasn't enough anymore for Tobias. Tobias wanted to be Tammy's husband and protector.

In between time, Tobias was happy to be at work. With a week's worth of Correction Officers' training, Tobias learned to become a better duty guard. Tobias took Self-defense, CPR, Fire prevention and assorted classes in preparation for his assigned duty task. He sat in his office confidently, knowing he had acquired the needed requirements to handle any inmate. Although, in certain cases, he still needed assistance during some instances but he felt adequate to handle situations alone. Mr. Bell made Tobias a visit. He informed Tobias; Inmate Julius still resided in his dorm. No changes had been made, as for his living arrangements. Except, the inmate would receive counseling on his behavior because he tried to commit suicide. Therefore, Julius was required to have 24-hours watch, until further notice.

Tobias made constant checks on Julius about every hour and documented what he witnessed. Inside a inmates' sleeping room consisted of a bunk bed and 2 personal inmate lockers. The rooms were secured by a steel locked door with a square window located on the door. The square window size was estimated at 1 foot in length and 1 foot in width. It was big enough, where Tobias could peep through and could observe all around inside the room. The doors were manually locked and unlocked by controls inside the Correction Officer's office or by a key. Tobias looked through the windows of the inmates' rooms; he witnessed the inmates sleeping on their bunk or snacking on their locker food. Except, when he reached inmate Brown and Julius room, the window was covered with black construction paper.

Without hesitation, Tobias knocked on the inmates' door and warn them about covering the window with paper. After the inmates had been warned of their wrong doings, Tobias escorted Julius out his room and secured his room door, while Brown was still locked in the room. Tobias had a private talk with Inmate Julius about his feelings. Julius informed to Tobias; he felt his life was in danger, if he continued to live in his present conditions. He wanted to be transferred to another Prison facility or he was going to kill himself. Therefore, Tobias asked Julius, "What was going on?" Julius notified his safety was in jeopardy, while he was room-mating with Inmate Brown. Therefore, Tobias informed Inmate Julius; he would notify the problem in his log and try to help him get a transfer.

Inmate Julius returned to his room unhappily. Afterwards, Tobias secured all the inmate rooms and returned to his office station. Tobias office phone rang and a notification from Mr. Bell came. They were having a potluck dinner for a few of the Correction Officers. Tobias was invited but he didn't cook often. So, he called Tammy for her help. Tammy agreed to help him cook collard greens and macaroni for the Prison's dinner. Tobias mind became filled with thoughts of Tammy and him being a family. He fantasized of the family life and a career at the prison. Then, Tobias realized it was time for him to make another safety check in the inmate living areas. Tobias opened the dorm door and heard a loud cry. He wondered where it came from. He tipped toe quietly through the inmate living areas.

Tobias heard a loud scream again. It was a loud scream and then, following crying and weeping. Sadness came to Tobias. It was not the sound, Tobias wanted to hear. Tobias easily and quietly walked up to Inmate Brown and Julius room. He peeped through the door window. Brown and Julius were naked and parading around in the room. Tobias franticly knocked on the room door. He shouted to Brown, this would be the first time and last time he would tell Inmate Brown about their unusual behavior. It was against prison rules for him to be out of uniform. They were completely naked, which was against the Prison rules. Tobias notified if he caught them again, doing unusual sex acts, then he would have to report it to his supervisor. Furthermore, they would have to be placed in segregation.

The unusual incidents which occurred in inmates' Brown and Julius' room, Tobias recorded in his logbook. Tobias received his replacement, but he didn't feel proud of the night's experience. He was the Booty Guard; but they didn't know of this. For other Correction Officers, they might didn't care with the incidents which happened on his watch. To Tobias, it was a real problem. Tobias hated any kind of unwanted sexual act. His sex phobia caused him to be this way. As Tobias arrived home and laid in bed, he prayed to have the power for to prevent any unwanted sexual offenses by anyone. It was Tobias passion as the Booty Guard. The next morning, he couldn't wait to arrive for work, so he could tell his inmates he was the Booty Guard. There wasn't going to be any sex violators on his watch.

Tobias arrived to work the next morning refreshed. As he entered his office, he read the duty logbook and noticed he had a guess in the building. The present Staff member who was maintaining the pods, told Tobias a counselor was counseling inmate Julius about his situation with his roommate. Therefore, Tobias hurried to do his inmate accountability to meet with the counselor. It was important for Tobias to make it known, Inmate Julius needed to be transfer for his health and safety. After the inmates were accounted and secured, Tobias relieved the other Staff member. Then, Tobias walked across the recreation area to the counselor's office. Tobias peeped inside the counselor's office and became surprised. It was Psychologist Pamela Sway, who helped Tobias get the Correction Officer's position.

Pamela Sway rushed out her office and told Tobias, could you excuse us while we discuss some important matters. Tobias being surprised said, "Hi Pamela! Oh sure, I can give you a couple of minutes alone with the inmate. Then, I would like to discuss some things with you also". Afterwards, Tobias walked across the pavement to his office. Tobias noticed Inmate Julius had his head down and was quiet. Julius looked as if he hadn't slept for a couple of nights and Pamela Sway was rubbing his shoulders as if giving him a massage. This was against standard Prison rules for counselors to touch inmates by physical contact. Although, Tobias knew the inmate was in a depressing situation. Albeit, Tobias still had to make the counselor aware of her wrong doings.

The counselors' meeting with Inmate Julius was about to come to an end. Tobias knew because the counselors' door was open and Tobias noticed the counselor and inmate standing up. Therefore, Tobias walked eagerly to the counselor's office. Pamela looked stunned to witness Tobias standing by her door. She looked at Tobias and then, she told Inmate Julius to be patient with further notice on his transfer. Maybe, something will happen soon. Inmate Julius departed and Tobias informed Pamela, hello again. The counselor asked Tobias, "How can she help?" Tobias informed he didn't know she was a Prison counselor. Pamela informed she did a lot, which he didn't know about. Tobias acknowledge, she was right; but he must advise her, not to touch the inmates, and he should be present in the office with the inmate.

Pamela explained to Tobias; she counsels inmates in complete confidentiality, to make the inmates feel trusted. Tobias begged the difference. He pleaded with Pamela not to talk to inmates alone. Although, it was the counselor's job to make all discussions with inmates confidential. Tobias told the counselor he felt helpless because he promised to be her Booty Guard, when seeing her. It was no help. Tobias even tried to plead with the Prison administration. The Prison Administration denied his request for him to be present during inmate's counseling. Altogether, Inmate Julius kept making appointment meetings to discuss matters with the counselor. Tobias felt frustrated with the meetings and decided to talk things over with the roommate Brown again.

So, Tobias made a discussion with Inmate Brown, during lockdown hours. Lockdown hours were all the inmates were secured in their rooms, during nighttime hours. The only inmate who was allowed out in the recreation yard, was the Inmate Brown. Tobias met with Inmate Brown and discussed, why he wants to harass Inmate Julius. Inmate Brown laughed and informed Inmate Julius was his girlfriend. Nobody was going to change his mind. Tobias asked Inmate Brown, "Was he gay?" Inmate Brown reported he was not gay; but he sometimes like to get his salad tossed. It was no joking matter to Tobias because sexual assaults were serious business. Tobias threaten the Inmate Brown. Tobias told Inmate Brown; he was going to turn him into somebody's girlfriend.

Inmate Brown became furious at the thought of Tobias threat. He pulled his pants down and peed on Tobias shoes. Tobias looked at Inmate Brown in his eyes and told him; he was going to make him pay for that. Inmate Brown was a big guy. He had broad shoulders and big fore arms. Every day, Inmate Brown would spend time in the recreation yard to exercise. Tobias was a big guy too; but he was young and Inmate Brown was a middle age man. He wasn't about to fight a grown man without some assistance. Inmate Brown asked Tobias, "Did he want a piece of him?" He told Tobias; he had already peed on his shoes. What's wrong with you, scared of me? Come on, let's fight! Tobias told him to wait. He walked in his office and made a call on his radio. Then, he opened the gate and 3 Correction Officers walked in.

Inmate Brown ran towards Tobias. With one blow, Tobias knocked him out. Tobias regretted doing this. He wasn't trying to make enemies with anyone at his job. Although, Inmate Brown deserved it. The 3 Correction Officers dragged Inmate Brown away. Then, Tobias had to appear for court in prison and explain, why he punched Inmate Brown. Nevertheless, the Prison court ruled in Tobias favor as self-defense. Furthermore, Inmate Brown became worser. Once Inmate Brown returned to his cell, he tortured Inmate Julius again, behind closed doors. Tobias couldn't stand to hear the torture, which Inmate Julius was going through. So, he promised to Inmate Julius, Inmate Brown would pay for all the abuse he dished out. Therefore, he talked to his Prison Sergeant for a favor.

Correction Officer Bell had become a Sergeant in the Prison cell. Tobias asked Sergeant Bell a favor because they had become friends. He asked Sergeant Bell, "Would he help Inmate Julius become transferred to another prison because the available rooms were full at this location?" Sergeant Bell informed he would try. Nevertheless, Tobias spent his lunch breaks mingling with Sergeant Bell. On occasions, Counselor Pamela Sway would attend the luncheons. Pamela Sway would ask Tobias about his extreme concerns for sex victims. Tobias notified the counselor; he was a sex victim before. His focus in life were to help sex victims of all cases. Sergeant Bell in joking, suggested he would assign all sex offenders to his building, where he could straighten them out because Tobias was a big guy.

Unfortunately, days went passing by and Inmate Julius was still residing in Tobias building pod. The counselor appeared at Tobias entrance gate. She reported some good news. The Inmate had gotten a notice by mail to the prison. Counselor Pamela Sway would tell the inmate in counseling; he was going to be exchanged in place for another inmate to a new prison facility. Tobias was overjoyed. He rushed to bring the Inmate up for counseling. Although, he knew not to tell or show the other inmates, which Inmate Julius was leaving. Tobias enter the Inmate living spaces. Other inmates were observing, so Tobias walked as normal because any sudden expression of joy would probably give it away. As Tobias arrived at Inmate Julius door, he whispered at the door, "Inmate Julius for meeting upstairs in counselor's office".

Inmate Julius opened the cell door. He smelled of feces, waste and body odor. The Prison room appeared to have been trashed. The inmate looked underfed and barely could move. Tobias looked in amazement because it was only days since he visually spoken to the inmate. He asked the inmate, "You okay and ready for the meeting?" Inmate Julius informed what meeting. Tobias told Julius; you have a meeting with the counselor now. Wake up inmate! The inmate informed Tobias; he doesn't care about no meeting. Tobias informed him; it is important. You better go. Inmate Julius looked at Inmate Brown. Inmate Brown smiled at Tobias. Julius informed Tobias, give him a couple of minutes to come out. Tobias waited by the Inmates door. Then, Julius decided to come out.

Tobias escorted Inmate Julius to the counselor's office. The counselor was happy to talk with the inmate. She informed the inmate to have a seat in her office. Then, she glanced at Tobias. Tobias told the counselor; excuse me for trespassing, I will leave you all some privacy. As Tobias began to walk away, he thought he heard a door close. Although, he wasn't for sure. The idea, which Inmate Julius was finally transferring, excited Tobias. A phone call was made from Tobias, at his office desk. Tobias waited for a couple of minutes for what he thought would be a celebration by Inmate Julius and Counselor Sway. Then, suddenly, 3 Correction Officers with Sergeant Bell rushed to his front gate. Sergeant Bell told Tobias, open his front gate quickly because they got an emergency notification.

Tobias opened his front gate. He questioned Sergeant Bell, what was the meaning of this emergence. Sergeant Bell informed Tobias; he would tell him later. Then, Sergeant Bell rushed to the counselor's office. Although, the door was closed and locked. Tobias looked through the little small window. He could feel vibrations through the door from Pamela's screams. Inmate Julius had one hand on the counselor's panties, while the counselor was bent over on the desk. The inmate was thrusting himself inside the counselor. Tobias quickly grabbed his door key and open the door. Pamela scream to the top of her lungs. Inmate Julius tried to escape but the 3 Correction Officers subdued the inmate. They placed a gigantic sub pressing shield on top of the inmate, where he couldn't move.

Tobias picked up Counselor Pamela Sway in his arms and carried her out the office. The counselor screamed and cried the entire moment. Sergeant Bell called for additional support, while medical staff carried the counselor out the prison. Inmate Julius barely escaped alive. Tobias kept punching the inmate, while he was subdued. Sergeant Bell informed Tobias; he did enough damage. Tobias thought, how could he allow this to happen. He was Counselor Sway's Booty Guard. Counselor Sway was his role model and friend. Then, Tobias trusted the inmate enough for him to receive help. Tobias thought, no wonder why not to trust inmates. Certainly, Inmate Julius would be transferred now. Although, it will not be to his comfort.

Nevertheless, Inmate Brown had a room to himself. Then, Inmate Julius was sent to a Top Secret-Security Prison in Raleigh, NC. For as Counselor Pamela Sway, she never returned to the City's Prison system. Furthermore, Sergeant Bell figured he would assign every sex molester to reside under Tobias with the reputation as the Booty Guard. Tobias wouldn't have knowledge of sex molesters or not. Although, it appeared, they gave themselves away by their actions. For example, Inmate Donald Round first stay was normal. The inmate had his personal items in a plastic trash bag as normal. Then, he sat at a table and inventoried everything in his bag. Inmate Round placed the stuff on the table. The last items inventoried was family pictures of his family.

Family pictures from an Inmate's family was common; but this inmate decided to put all the children pictures in a pile. Then, Inmate Round began kissing the pictures and smelling them. Inmate Round would touch the pictures, then touch himself in his private area. Other inmates, including Inmate Brown watched. Inmate Brown asked him, "Did he like touching the children's pictures?" Inmate Round laugh and said, "Yes!" His laughter got louder and he said "Yes" again. Then, the yes got louder. Inmate Brown informed to Inmate Round; this is great because he liked touching too. Tobias shouted, "Okay, inmates quiet down; and inmates put the pictures away!" Then, Tobias walked towards him and whispered, "Who are these children, who you are kissing inmate?" The inmate informed, they are my Aunt's and Uncle's children. Then, some are my ex-supervisor's children.

From further investigating by Tobias, Inmate Round was in his late sixties and divorced. Inmate Round was an ex-politician worker and worked for a State Congressman. He lived his life with privileges and got what he wanted most of the time. Except, Inmate Round messed up. Inmate Round fooled with the wrong person's child. Unfortunately, he got locked up in jail with bad health and overweight. Sadly, Inmate Round lost all his benefits. Next, Inmate Round lost his wife and children, which probably was for the best. Peradventure, Inmate Round was molesting his own nephews and nieces. Soon, Inmate Round didn't have anyone to depend on. Except, Inmate Round had one friend, who he helped reach prominent status. Also, this friend was very loyal to Inmate Round's needs.

Therefore, Tobias thoughts about Inmate Round kissing children, brought strange looks on Tobias' face. Inmate Brown looked at Tobias. Then, he said, "Yes, he molested these kids. I heard he molested these kids. He had sex with them and everything". Tobias looked strange at Inmate Brown. Therefore, Inmate Brown said, "Allow him to be my roommate. I will show him some love, as he showed these children love. Yes, I enjoy showing love". Tobias looked at Inmate Brown again. Then, he told Inmate Round, "For now on your roommate will be Inmate Brown". Inmate Round looked at Tobias and said, "No, no way!" Tobias said, "Yes, yes way! Albeit, you have a good stay Inmate Round". Tobias walked away and locked everyone in their assigned rooms.

Before Tobias was relieved of duty, he heard a scream from Inmate Round inside his room. So, Tobias decided to check on Inmate Round. Tobias knocked on Inmate Round's door. Inmate Brown peeped through the window of the door inside their room. Tobias asked Brown, "Was everything okay?" Inmate Brown informed it will be. Therefore, Tobias advised Inmate Brown to only scare him with a show of force. Although, do not treat Inmate Round with sexual mistreatment or harm. Inmate Brown frowned and informed Tobias; don't worry because the inmate wasn't his type. Although, Inmate Round would have learned a lesson, not to sexually abuse any children again. Tobias acknowledge to Inmate Brown; very good. Then, he peeped through the window at Inmate Round. The Inmate was curled up on his sleeping bunk and shivering scared.

Tobias heard on the radio; his relief was waiting for him at the gate. So, Tobias gave Inmate Brown a warning, for him not to harm Inmate Round. Furthermore, he will see him later tonight. Next, he rushed to the gate, so he could be relieved. It was Sergeant Bell at the gate. Sergeant Bell informed Tobias; he should apply for Sergeant because he had the prudential to fill the position. Tobias was amazed to hear of this. He informed he would think about it. Then, Tobias departed for home. As Tobias arrived at home, a strange vehicle was in his parents' driveway. It was a fancy Lincoln Town car. Tobias parents opened their front door and the City Mayor was seated at the breakfast bar drinking coffee.

Tobias walked into his home, while everyone else was talking about the District and the hopes of improving the area. Unfortunately, W-S Prime Motel was becoming a place for sex solicitation. It was an election year for the Mayor and the District was causing him concerns. The Mayor reported the Chief of Police was running negative campaigns against him because he was running for Mayor. Furthermore, the W-S Prime Motel Manager Mr. Williams was campaigning for the Chief of Police. Dislike was shown on the Mayor's face. Therefore, he asked Tobias, "Did any unlawful activities occurred?" Tobias told the Mayor; he did know about some criminal activity going on, when he worked at the motel. Although, he was a prison guard now. So, he didn't know anything about the W-S Prime Motel now.

A vibrating sound occurred on Tobias cell phone. It was Tammy calling for Tobias. She acted as if it was an extreme importance. So, Tobias excused himself in front of the Mayor, while everyone else kept discussing about W-S Prime's Motel problems. Tobias answered the phone and Tammy informed him; the bank where she works has approved her for a business loan. Therefore, she wanted him to attend dinner with her at the W-S Prime Motel Bar. Tobias asked her, "Why the W-S Prime Motel Bar?" Tammy informed him; it was a place, which she was about to become part ownership. She notified Tobias; Sherri and she were buying the bar because strange and dangerous events have been happening. The female staff operator had been requiring female workers to perform sexual request from clients.

Tobias in astonishment told Tammy; he wished her good luck and congratulations on her soon to be new business ownership. He informed Tammy; he surely would be there at the dinner because it would be a memorial occasion. Besides, he would have to be their Booty Guard because as business owners, they would need the service. Tammy informed Tobias; she needs the booty guard service because they were a couple now. Tobias notified Tammy; he needed to meet with her and gather more information about the bar because he had been out of touch with his prison job. Therefore, he would speak to her another time in person. Furthermore, Tobias and Tammy made their goodbyes and ended their talk. Then, Tobias returned to his family and the Mayor, to report the new news.

When Tobias greeted his family and the Mayor, they were still discussing the motel. Tobias told the Mayor; he thinks there is a clue, which the motel was conducting prostitution, solicitation and sex trafficking. The Mayor looked with great enthusiasm. He wanted to know everything and the resource of where it was coming from. Tobias acknowledge to the Mayor; he couldn't give him any information, until he was confident, it was real. Ms. Elle and Mr. Rogers believed they needed to scout the W-S Prime Motel for sex workers because they had prior experience with sex trafficking. Also, Mr. Rogers and the Motel Manager Mr. Williams were old associates. Although, Tobias pleaded he would handle the investigation alone. Tobias informed the Mayor; if he finds any criminal activity at the motel, then the Mayor would be notified first by phone.

The City Mayor departed the home of Tobias' parents in a hopeful mood, which his chances of staying Mayor still had possibilities. The Chief of Police was running a successful campaign so far as a new campaign Mayor. So, he had become confident of winning. Therefore, the Police Chief had already made plans at the W-S Prime Motel of an event party and inviting his most supportive police, fire fighters and emergency medical workers. A phone call was made to Helen, who had become his loyal mistress. The Police Chief wanted to make sure, his event party had all the ingredients to having a party good. Therefore, Helen notified her mother Nostalgia. Then, Nostalgia sent letters to her personal sex workers, which were working undercover as motel female staff. Accidentally, Sherri got a letter.

Sherri got a letter certified by Nostalgia, informing the female staff workers at the bar to dress in their provocative attire on a certain night because motel customers will be paying for sex entertainment. Therefore, it was their duty to provide sexual pleasures for motel customers to obtain their business. Furthermore, since it was city workers who were being service, no judgements would be given. Also, additional checks would be provided to female staff for giving sexual favors to city workers and no harm would be done. Then, Sherri complained about the letter, so Nostalgia told her; opportunities to make extra money don't come this easy. So, take advantage and don't complain.

Then, Sherri told Tammy about the letter. Tammy told Tobias; the W-S Prime Bar female workers were required to give sexual favors to the City workers of Winston Salem. Therefore, Tobias informed the City Mayor; Motel female staff workers would be given sex favors to the City Workers of Winston-Salem, NC because they were paid and advised to do so. Then, the City Mayor told Tobias about the history of the sex trafficking at W-S Prime Bar. The City Mayor informed Tobias; his father Mr. Russel worked for him. Therefore, Mr. Russel and Ms. Elle needed travel assistance for Motel female workers of the W-S Prime Motel. The Motel Bar was their gathering place. Mr. Russel Nelson contacted the Mayor because he operated the airport. Therefore, he could provide an escape route for the female workers.

CHAPTER 6

Save the booties

TAMMY INFORMED TOBIAS; SHE ALSO made plans to have a celebration with her High School classmates to celebrate her part ownership of the W-S Prime Bar. Therefore, Tobias attended the celebration of the new part ownership of the Winston Salem Prime Bar. Now, the W-S Prime Bar operated independently from the motel. Helen continued to supervise the female waiting staff, while Sherri controlled operations in the kitchen. Then, Ricky worked as Motel Security. The operation appeared to be working well, until it was time for the City Workers Galilee Ball. Then, Tammy and Sherri's celebration wasn't too much a happy occasion after all. Suddenly, Tobias arrived as Tammy's Booty Guard. Then, Tammy's classmates arrived and Ricky, Persia, Mercedes, Melvin, Tracy with Craig entered.

Persia who became a college football player talked about how he needed Tobias to protect him from the college girls. He admitted to Tobias because of football fame, it was difficult for him to study and keep good grades. Therefore, he wished he had the booty guard protection. Tracy and Craig who were Social workers wished they had the booty guard protection too because they had relationship trust issues with each other. Melvin wanted the booty guard duty to protect him from the paparazzi. Finally, Mercedes missed having her cousin as the Booty Guard because she became popular as a Radio Broadcaster. Peradventure, it kept Mercedes with bad company consisting of creepy man. Nevertheless, most of them requested to hire Tobias as the Booty Guard. Tobias told them, he worked at the prison now. Although, he might consider doing them a favor.

Respectfully, after the celebration, the classmates began leaving. Then, Sherri cried. Tobias asked Sherri, "What was wrong?" So, Tammy informed Tobias; Sherri was having problems at work and needed the booty guard duty. Tobias recapped he was only the Booty Guard for her and his job. Although, Tammy informed Tobias; Sherri really needed him because she recognized the sex crimes in her workplace. Then, no one was doing anything about it. Even her boyfriend Ricky seemed to look the other way. Sherri, then informed Mr. Williams and Nostalgia were operating a sex operation and needed to be stop. So, Tobias comforted Sherri; then informed he would see what he could do to stop the sex crimes as the Booty Guard. Therefore, Sherri should act normal and keep their conversation a secret.

Tobias returned to work at the City Prison. He had worked at the Prison for almost a year now. So, he no longer considered himself new anymore. As Tobias entered his work area through the main gate, prisoners were gathered in the recreation yard. Therefore, Tobias sent them back to their sleeping areas. Noise from chatter and talk were coming from the counselors' office. A curiosity from Tobias occurred. Inmate Donald Round began backing out of the counselor's office, while the counselor was counseling him about a transfer. Tobias watched as they approached him. Then, he told the counselor, it was inmate lock down time. Inmate lock down time was the time for inmates to be secured in their beds. So, the counselor who was now a guy, informed it was fine. They were finished with everything.

Inmate Donald Round departed to his room. Tobias secured both his inmate pods living area. Then, he escorted the counselor through the main gate. Although, before he opened the gate, he commented about Inmate Round transferring. The counselor informed Tobias; he didn't' know. Peradventure, if so, he would receive a notice on his desk. Tobias locked the main gate behind the counselor. Then, he rushed inside the pod, where Inmate Round resided. As Tobias entered the pod, Inmate Round was sitting at a table. Inmate Round informed him; he was waiting for him. Tobias asked Inmate Round, "You are leaving us now?" Inmate Round informed Tobias; hopefully because he had learned a lesson. He loved children so much and only, wanted to show them love.

Although, Inmate Round didn't know how to show love because he never was really loved. Inmate Round thought he knew how to give love to children but he didn't. He was sexually abused by his uncle at an early age. Therefore, this was the only love Inmate Round knew, how to give children. This was what Inmate Round experienced. Inmate Brown told Inmate Round; his love was inappropriate, and he deserved to be disciplined for his actions. Then, he beat the crap out of Inmate Round. Eventually, Inmate Round learned how to give love to children, but not with sex. It was by showing of care for the children's safety and economic survival. Inmate Round cried in joy for his transformation with ending his sex addition for children. He thanked Tobias as the Booty Guard and Inmate Brown for his recovery.

Then, the next day, Tobias realized Inmate Donald Round was gone. Therefore, a different inmate became roommate's with Inmate Brown. Tobias looked at the inmate. It was a Black guy. The Black guy's name was Franklyn. He was conversing with Inmate Brown steadily. Tobias was listening to Inmate Franklyn gossip about his girlfriends on the street. Franklyn described how he smacked his girlfriends, when they tried to get out of control. Furthermore, he was a street pimp and his business became tricking the women into prostituting, while they were afraid of him. Then, he would obtain a share of their money for protecting them. Although, if they talked to Franklyn unkindly, then he would demonstrate a show of displeasure. So, Franklyn bragged about his street credit, which he had on the street to Inmate Brown.

Franklyn wanted to impress Tobias good. Therefore, he approached Tobias nicely. Then, Franklyn told Tobias, he heard of him being an expert prison guard and a fair prison guard. So, Franklyn believed he could work out a deal with Tobias. The deal was for Tobias to allow phone calls being made on a cell phone. In exchange, Franklyn would introduce Tobias to his prostitutes on the street. Tobias told Franklyn; he had a girlfriend already. Inmate Brown was listening to Franklyn's conversation and shook his head. He asked Franklyn, "Did he enjoy forcing decent woman to become prostitutes?" Inmate Franklyn informed Brown; he enjoyed it. They would do anything he said. Then, he laughed. Furthermore, his laugh got louder. Therefore, Tobias shook his head and informed Franklyn, to return to his cell.

Inmate Brown looked at Tobias. Tobias returned the favor. He informed Brown; something needed to be done about Inmate Franklyn. Nobody needs to be walking around and thinking, it is fine to manipulate woman into selling sex. Inmate Brown acknowledged to Tobias; it's okay, Sir. He was going to handle it. This was his roommate. So, he would handle it. Later, Inmate Franklyn showed an address book full of numbers and references. Then, he informed Tobias; this name right here in his address book, was his best friend, mentor and father figure. Tobias asked Franklyn, "Where was this man now?" Franklyn informed Tobias, he was locked up at this prison. Tobias asked Franklyn, "Why didn't he teach you how to stay out of prison?" Franklyn informed Tobias, the man got locked up for operating a business to solicit prostitution. The name of Billy Prime had 4 stars beside it.

Tobias informed Inmate Brown; he wanted him to touch up on Inmate Franklyn badly. He told Inmate Brown; he heard some terrible stories from Franklyn. The stories of abuse, manipulation and belittlement, which were heard from Inmate Franklyn's mouth, were the techniques he used to cause women to prostitute because they had no encouragement from anybody. So, Tobias caused a sentence of pain to Franklyn. Tobias told Inmate Brown for whatever cost, make him suffer. Then, Franklyn would have wished he never caused any harm to them women. Therefore, Inmate Brown thought for a long while. Inmate Brown told Tobias; this would cost him heavy because the Inmate have important friends. Tobias acknowledge to Inmate Brown; he didn't care about any of Inmate Franklyn's important friends he had in the prison system.

Tobias told Inmate Brown; he follows, what he tells him or he was going to make him a girlfriend for an inmate. Therefore, Inmate Brown became upset. Later during the early morning, Tobias heard a hollering and screaming from Inmate Franklyn. Although, Tobias ignored the noises. Then, Correction Officers with Sergeant Bell rushed to Tobias' perimeter main gate. Sergeant Bell directed Tobias to open his perimeter main gate and inmate pod living areas. Tobias asked Sergeant Bell, "What was happening?" Sergeant Bell informed Tobias; he would tell him later. Therefore, Tobias did what he was told. Later, Sergeant Bell and the other Correction Officers carried Inmate Franklyn out of the room naked and lifeless. Tobias with opened eyes and wide mouth became apologetic for being nonchalant.

Tobias informed to Sergeant Bell; he was sorry and took full responsibility for the inmate's condition. He was the Booty Guard and it was his job to prevent sexual incidents. Inmate Brown looked with curiosity. Sergeant Bell informed Tobias; it's okay. Everyone knows who did it. Tobias, it's okay! Tobias was in complete shock and bewildered. Then, Sergeant Bell and the other Correction Officers departed the area with the body of Inmate Franklyn. Furthermore, Tobias locked the main perimeter gate behind them. Tobias entered the pod, which housed the sleeping area of Inmate Brown. He asked Inmate Brown, "What was your problem? Why did you kill Inmate Franklyn?" Inmate Brown informed Tobias; Inmate Franklyn didn't want to conform because he was a pimp. So, he made Inmate Franklyn his girlfriend because it was the one thing, which he mostly feared.

Tobias sat down beside Inmate Brown's room door and thought for a minute. Then, he informed Inmate Brown, he understood him. Although, they might have to pay for their bad behavior. It was worse than suicide for a Correction Officer in a building, if an inmate dies on their watch. Furthermore, if an inmate caused it, then it was a life of damnation for the inmate. Tobias showed up for work the next day and Inmate Brown was gone. There was no message or notice of his well-being. Tobias was called up for a meeting. When he returned to his building, an inmate who was big and tall with a serious disposition, was waiting in Inmate Brown's room. The man was a Caucasian man in his late sixties or early seventies. He asked Tobias, "Would you be the man they called the Booty Guard?"

Tobias informed the inmate; who might you be. The man told Tobias, his name was Billy Prime and Inmate Franklyn's mentor. Tobias stared at Billy. He informed to Billy; Yes, I am the Booty Guard. Billy looked with wide eyes and a big grin. He spoke, "What a tragedy, for someone's life would be wasted and for no reason at all. If only people would do their jobs properly". Tobias asked, "How so?" Billy informed Tobias; life was a game of chances, why it was best to be skilled at your game. Tobias informed Billy, it really depends on the game you are playing because no one should be sexually manipulated or bullied. Billy told Tobias, everyone becomes used for something at one point; and sex is no different. Tobias informed Billy, he was a religious man. He didn't believe in sexual manipulation.

Billy explained to Tobias; he ran a business for over 20 years. He operated a restaurant, motel and nightclub. Although, what his customers appreciated the most was sex and good hospitality of his female staff workers. Men and women would flock to his motel, so they could be greeted by a warm and friendly motel staff. Billy informed Tobias, what he offered was something no one else did. He offered a night of love and kindness. Therefore, over dozens of pretty women would train and work hard, so others would experience love. It was the sacrifice of others, which allowed certain individuals to be filled with joy. Billy preached to Tobias; every business was a servant for man's betterment. Therefore, the sex trade was no different. It was a sacrifice, which one gave for the betterment of all.

Tobias asked Billy, "Where was this business located because he might have heard about this business?" Billy informed Tobias, he should because his business was operated in the heart of the District. Tobias stood taller and looked at Billy. Then, he asked Billy, "Who would believe this foolishness?" Billy informed Tobias; he had customers from everywhere and including important clients, who still participated in this tradition. Tobias asked Billy, "You are trying to say, you once owned the W-S Prime Motel and they have a tradition of keeping prostitutes for customers. Billy looked at Tobias with a glance. Then, he informed Tobias; he was talking to Billy Prime and the man who put the District on the map. The District's reputation started from him. Although, other Motel managers have been copycats, who followed his instructions on how to operate W-S Prime Motel and Bar.

Tobias discussion with Billy Prime gave him a lot of information. Therefore, he told Billy Prime, good day Sir. There were no more further questions for him. So, Tobias sent Billy Prime to his room. Although, not without Billy asking Tobias, "Who killed my companion Franklyn because someone was going to pay dearly?" Nevertheless, when Tobias shift ended, he spoke to the City Mayor. Tobias explained to the Mayor; he had a sure bet, which prostitution would be going on at the City Galilee Ball because of a prisoner named Billy Prime. The Mayor asked Tobias, "Where did he get to meet Billy Prime from?" Tobias informed the Mayor; he met Billy Prime in prison. The Mayor informed Tobias, to stay away from him. The man was extremely dangerous and not to be taken likely. Tobias acknowledge to the Mayor; he knew because Billy Prime was in prison.

Albeit, the Mayor informed persistently. Tobias do not converse with Billy Prime in any manner. The man was a liar, manipulator and a crook among other things. So, beware of the Devil, being Billy Prime as the Devil. Therefore, Tobias informed the Mayor; it was okay because he knows where helpful information was located about city employees who purchase and consumed with the business of prostitutes. Furthermore, he would hopefully handover an address book from a well-known inmate named Franklyn, which list all the wrong doers. Unfortunately, the inmate was no longer alive; and he would not be socializing with Billy Prime anymore. The City Mayor informed to Tobias; rest his sole. What an unfortunate tragedy to die in a penitentiary. He must inform his love ones with a respectable explanation of his death. Tobias informed to Mayor; yes, sure Sir.

The next day, Tobias arrived for work. As Tobias relieved the departing Correction Officer, a group of disgruntled inmates approached him. They were upset because they believed he ordered Inmate Brown to kill Inmate Franklyn. A riot broke out. It was Inmate Billy Prime leading the group. Tobias locked himself up in his office. Then, he called Sergeant Bell for help. Sergeant Bell arrived with more Correction Officers. Furthermore, he relieved Tobias with a message. Tobias had to report to the Prison Warden. Once Tobias arrived in front of the Prison Warden, the City Mayor was present. The Prison Warden gave him the unfortunate message, which he was suspended with pay, until he appeared in court about Inmate Franklyn's death.

Therefore, Tobias had plenty of available time now. He began concentrating on the W-S Prime Motel City Galilee Ball. He notified Tammy; he was suspended from his job until he had a court appearance. The City Galilee was happening in 5 days, which was fortunate for Tobias because he was out of work. With all the available time, Tobias figured he would surprise his friends and do some booty guard service. Tobias notified Tammy; he was going to be her Booty Guard for today. Tammy worked as a Banking Agent. So, Tobias waited behind a customer, before he was able to speak to Tammy. The customer was talking rude and inappropriate to Tammy. Tobias overheard the customer suggest, Tammy and he meet privately in her break room.

Tobias attracted Tammy's attention suddenly, without any notice from the customer. Then, Tobias gave a clue to Tammy, he was going to the breakroom too. Tobias pointed his index finger in the direction of the breakroom. Unfortunately, the customer did not witness Tobias because his back was facing him. By the time, Tammy and the customer sat down in the breakroom, Tobias appeared. The customer assumed Tammy and he would be alone. Although, it was not the case. Tobias walked up behind him and touch him on the shoulder. The man asked Tobias, "What was the meaning of this?" Tobias informed the customer; he was the Booty Guard. Then, if he had any thoughts of trying to receive some booty, he had caused an error. Banking issues was what she did.

The customer stood up and looked at Tobias. He clearly realized Tobias meant business and he had made a big mistake. Tammy asked the customer, "Sir, do you want to do business with this bank?" The customer informed Tammy; yes! Please set me up a certificate of deposit account. Tammy acknowledge the customer with a "Thank you and have a good day". Then, Tobias escorted the customer out the bank with one arm behind his back. Shortly afterwards, Tobias returned inside the bank. Tobias kissed Tammy. Tammy told Tobias, thank you. Tobias asked Tammy, "Do the businessman named Billy Prime own business loans to this bank?" Tammy informed Tobias; Billy Prime still owes the bank money for real estate property in the District. Tobias informed Tammy, interesting. Now, Tobias knew Billy Prime was still in debt with the bank.

Tammy informed Tobias; W-S Prime Motel and Bar were becoming stranger because unknown women have been showing up as part of the female work staff. The kitchen cooks are fine because they are standard people; but the female waiting staff, house cleaning and desk clerks are mostly new who are females. Helen has been doing her best to train them. Although, it has been difficult for her to establish good quality service for customers. The new female staff are pretty and unique but their hospitality skills are poor. Tobias informed Tammy, it was what he predicted. Nostalgia was bringing in female workers who were probably in disguised as hospitality workers but, were nothing more than street prostitutes. Tobias figured it was a job for the Booty Guard.

The next day, he decided to visit Melvin's workplace. Melvin was in the process of delivering fashion clothing to a local department store. Tobias notified Melvin; he was arriving but he was greeted with unwelcoming company. An anti-gay and lesbian hate group began threatening Melvin's attire. There were paparazzi present and taking pictures of his presence. Tobias noticed Melvin leaving out the exit door. Therefore, he ran to greet Melvin. Then, Melvin grabbed Tobias arm. Suddenly, Tobias was escorted by Melvin to his transportation van. The van was colorful with red, pink and black trim. A slogan on the van read "The Melvin Way". It was short but sweet and fitted Melvin's personality. Then a person in the hate group, grabbed Melvin's arm harshly.

An anti-gay man tried to tear Melvin's clothes off. Apparently, the man didn't like Melvin's half top fitting shirt or his tight-fitting shorts. Bible verses were being quoted and showed for protest, until the camera men started taking pictures of Melvin coming out the building. Then, the hate group became rowdy. Therefore, when the man grabbed Melvin, Tobias panicked and gave the disgruntled man a powerful punch. Afterwards, Tobias shouted to the crowd, "Please, keep your hands to yourselves everyone! This is a respectable man, who obviously will be important in life. A man who has done nothing wrong but created a fashionable, stylish attire which was in big demand. So, please allow this man to conduct his business!" Simultaneously, everyone moved back and the van speeded with Tobias and Melvin inside. Melvin informed thanks Tobias.

Therefore, on another day, Tobias notified Persia; he would report to his College University to spend a day with him as the Booty Guard. Persia was excited considering Tobias and him occasionally had their issues in the past. Although, he tried to make Tobias feel welcoming in the beginning. Tobias got a chance to go on a college tour from Persia. Then, Persia showed the football field to Tobias. They communicated about High School football and the trials of the football team. At one point, Tobias and Persia were on the football field and a college newspaper reporter recognized Persia. So, he met Persia for a personal interview. Albeit, other spectators began recognizing Persia as well. College girls ambushed Persia with hugs and kisses. Persia responded to Tobias by requesting his booty guard service.

Tobias in disbelief asked Persia, "You have College girls acting like this and you want me to stop it?" Persia informed Tobias; Yes. Tobias informed Persia; unbelievable because he thought it was his dream to have women treating him like a celebrity. Persia informed he use too. Although, now, he witnessed this too much. For Persia, it was becoming overwhelming. Persia asked Tobias, "Please, can you make them go away?" Tobias informed to Persia; okay! He began pulling the girls away from Persia. Then, a College girl asked Tobias, "Who do you supposed to be, his security guard?" Tobias informed with disgust; no, I am his Booty Guard. He only handled sexual assaults. To Tobias, it was clearly a job for the Booty Guard because Persia should have lost all his booty. The College women looked like models. Persia informed to Tobias; thank you!

Then, Tobias gave booty guard service to his cousin Mercedes. Tobias notified Mercedes; he would spend time with her, while she was soliciting an Advertisement commercial to a client. The Advertisement Manager appeared to be nice. Albeit, he carried himself smart and rich. Except, the Advertisement Manager was promoting Viagra, which Tobias didn't like. Therefore, Tobias kept quiet, until the Advertisement Manager became provocative sexually to Mercedes. So, Tobias interrupted the meeting. Tobias informed the Advertisement manager; he was wrong for using sexual language and unethical remarks. The Advertisement manager wanted to have sex with Mercedes. Tobias shouted, "Meeting was over with because the Booty Guard didn't believe in sexual enhancements because it might cause unfavorable sexual encounters".

Mercedes informed Tobias; her job was weird because she had to deal with situations as this. Tobias notified her; he was the Booty Guard. He protected all inappropriate sexual behavior to someone. Regardless, if it was on the job or at home. Tobias wasn't ashamed of his feelings because he believed in sexual restraint. Love came before sex and should be taught by counselors and the clergy. Tobias was Mercedes' Booty Guard, until she decided for him to stop. He was loyal to his family. Furthermore, he stayed with her during the entire morning radio show, while she made jokes and they laughed. Then, Tobias escorted her to his parents' home. At home, Tobias prepared himself by meditation and reading the Bible scriptures.

Surprisingly, Tobias woke up the next day feeling great. Tobias believed he had served some of his friends good with the booty duty. Albeit, he was not through because the couples were last. Therefore, Tracy and Craig were next on his list. Then, next, Tobias would help Sherry and Ricky last. A phone call was made to notify Tobias presence. Craig waited at his office for Tobias. As Tobias arrived, he noticed women employees socializing at Craig's desk. The women weren't talking about business and they were laughing. One woman was resting her arm on Craig's shoulder. Although, Craig was clearly focus on the other woman's legs because she had on a short skirt. Craig was smiling from ear to ear. Then, he recognized Tobias standing at a short distance, watching him.

Tobias frowned at Craig. Craig informed the women to give him a little privacy, while he talks to an old friend. Tobias asked Craig, "Where is your mate? She is supposed to be here?" Craig informed Tobias; she is on a road call. Tracy will be here in a minute. Tobias shook his head and informed Craig; you told me about some trust issues. Craig acknowledge to Tobias; Yes! Tobias instructed Craig; you must get rid of socializing with the female employees. It doesn't look good Craig. Now, if Tracy had walked in, then no Booty Guard could help you. Please Craig, help yourself and relationship. Then, Tobias informed the women in Craig's office to stay to themselves. He was the Booty Guard promoting safe sex and abstinence. Then, he informed the women; Craig was close to married.

Quietly, Tracy walked inside the office. Tobias didn't notice Tracy in the office. Tobias kept repeating to the women; Craig was obligated to a beautiful woman named Tracy who works in the building. They are almost married and have been dating for a good while. So, do not flirt with Craig. A woman informed Tobias; Craig doesn't have money anyways. The man works with us for Social Service. Tobias informed the woman; Yes, right. He barely can take care of his girlfriend. Tracy walked over to Craig and gave him a hug. Tobias turned around and noticed them hugging. He informed everyone; the Booty Guard has completed his task once again. If anyone needs booty guard duties, then ask Craig or Tracy because they have experience from High School.

It was a good day for Tobias. Until, Tobias got a wakeup call from the Mayor. The Mayor asked Tobias; "Have you been making plans to keep watch of the Chief of Police because they will be celebrating in the W-S Prime Motel, after the City Galilee Ball. The Police Chief thinks, he has wrapped up the Mayor seat. He will be getting drunk with his employees and others, while carousing with the Motel prostitutes. Tobias informed the Mayor; not on my watch Sir. If he does, you will receive a phone call immediately. The Booty Guard has a mission to stop all sexual misconduct from anyone. So, a date has been made with a High School friend to assist him with the booty duty. The Mayor informed Tobias; he was no longer an employee of W-S Prime Motel. Therefore, he must be careful.

After the end of the call with the Mayor, Tobias occurred another phone call by the City Prison. It was the Prison Warden informing him he had a court appearance the following week about Franklyn. Instructions were given to Tobias over the phone as he was summoned to court for 2nd degree murder of Inmate Franklyn. They say, Inmate Brown was threatened by you and in fear, while he killed Inmate Franklyn. Tobias knew it was a lie. He wondered who would benefit from Franklyn's death. Franklyn and Billy Prime were business partners and friends. Although, Billy Prime cared only about money and was crooked. So, Tobias wanted to know, did he owe Franklyn as well to the Winston-Salem District Bank. He made a phone call to Tammy.

Expectedly, Tammy informed Tobias; Billy Prime's Bank account had been emptied, while he was in prison. None of his assets had been paid by him. They were paid by a man named Mr. Williams. Therefore, Mr. Williams was maintaining Billy Prime's assets; and probably, Franklyn wasn't receiving no money. So, Tobias called Sergeant Bell to find out if Inmate Brown had a roommate who he socialized with regularly. Sergeant Bell told Tobias; he socialized solely with this gay prisoner on the close-security floor in the City Prison. Tobias informed Sergeant Bell; he needs to talk with Inmate Brown's roommate because he might have information on Inmate Brown. Therefore, Sergeant Bell gathered information from Inmate Brown's roommate.

Sergeant Bell notified Tobias; Inmate Brown's roommate told him, which Inmate Brown was paid by Billy Prime to kill Franklyn. Billy Prime couldn't afford to take care of Franklyn anymore. So, he had Franklyn killed. Tobias cried for joy. He then, notified Sergeant Bell to confiscate Franklyn's address book because it was important information for the Mayor. He would pick it up before his court date and hand carry it to the Mayor's office. Therefore, Tobias felt easy about his court appearance because he had nothing to do with Franklyn's death. So, he kept his mind on the City Galilee Ball. It was showcased the next day. So, he called Ricky to informed him about his presence. Ricky answered the call from Tobias. He was surprised. Tobias told Ricky; he was lucky because he has free booty guard service tomorrow.

Ricky explained to Tobias; he didn't need the Booty Guard. He had no celebrity problems, paparazzi, crazy client, trust issues with a wife or sex predator chasing after him. The only issue Ricky had was making more money because Motel Security Manager didn't pay a lot of money. So, Mr. Williams began paying Ricky additionally to keep him quiet about the sex solicitation in the motel. Tobias arrived in his best dressed attire. He notified Ricky; Sherri suggested assistance because customers might be flirting with him and her. Therefore, Ricky allowed Tobias to be his assistant. There were prostitution flyers advertising to government employees of an exciting good time from high class professional female care servants. Tobias managed to pick up Franklyn's address book from prison. So, all he had to do was call a number and pretend he was soliciting female sex workers.

After the City Employee Galilee Ball was over, Tobias mingled with Ricky for a few minutes. Then, he informed Ricky; he had to go check on Sherri. Therefore, he had a little free time to roam the Motel. Tobias didn't worry about the Staff Management because they were busy. Mr. Williams was hosting the event; Nostalgia was monitoring room keys for the guest and Helen was entertaining the Police Chief. This left Ricky and the security staff to make routine checks. Tobias felt it wasn't enough security on board inside the motel. Therefore, he made his own rounds. Tobias checked all 13 floors. Besides house cleaning who were female prostitutes laughing in the hallways, the Motel had no real violations. So, Tobias took the address book and called.

Tobias called each number slowly. The City employees would answer their phone; and Tobias would ask them, "Are you having a good time in the Motel? If not, then he could send them a pretty girl who could enjoy their time". Then, the customer would say, "Sure! Just put it on my motel bill". Then, Tobias circled the names of the clients. Tobias got ready to call the Mayor. Although, Tobias met Helen with the City Police Chief strolling to a Motel room. Helen pretended as if she didn't recognize Tobias but he knew she did because of her stare she made directly at him. As Tobias seen them go inside the Motel Room, he placed his head beside the door and heard laughing and carousing. Tobias shook his head in displeasure. Then he found a quiet area to call the Mayor.

The Mayor asked Tobias, "What was he seeing. Tobias informed the Mayor; men buying service workers. Prostitutes parading the motel. Also, City employees in motel rooms expecting to receive sex for a fee. The City Mayor informed Tobias; he did a good job. The State Patrol Officers were own their way to arrest anyone purchasing the service of prostitution or expecting to receive a prostitute. Therefore, Mr. Williams and his family would be arrested for operating a motel for soliciting women. Tobias ended the call of his cell phone, when he heard the State Patrol arrive. Then, he observed a large transportation vehicle arriving to pick up the female service workers who denied participating in prostitution. Mr. Rogers and Ms. Elle Nelson help assist the female service workers in the vehicle. Tobias was amazed but not surprised.

The next day, Tobias heard they arrested Mr. Williams, Nostalgia and Helen for operating a motel to conduct prostitution. The City Police Chief lost his election to Mayor. Sherry thanked Tobias eventually, for her day to be protected by the Booty Guard. Ricky came around and thanked Tobias for his assistance too. When Tobias arrived for court, they prosecuted Billy Prime for 2nd degree murder and Inmate Brown was charged with 1st degree murder. The Prison Warden relocated both the prisoners. Therefore, Tobias reported to work at his normal workplace. Albeit, Tobias was placed with a different inmate in his custody. Then, Tobias was informed; the inmate was a companion of Inmate Brown. Also, the inmate helped Inmate Brown get the plea deal and free Tobias from prosecution. So, Tobias was eager to meet the inmate.

Tobias rushed to open the pod, where the inmate resided. The inmate was a Caucasian inmate, tall and bald. He kept shouting football signals. The inmate repeated blue and gray, slant 20, slant 20, said hut, hut, hut. Then, other inmates shouted,

"Inmate Coach please be quiet. Please, Coach be just a little quieter. The Correction Officer will be coming through". Tobias stared at the Inmate. Then, Tobias recognized it was Coach Johnson from his High School. Tobias didn't use profound language because Coach Johnson never liked cussing. He only implied, "they done gave him another one to break. When will Sergeant Bell give him a break". Therefore, Tobias greeted Inmate Johnson with a "Welcome Coach. Together, we be again".

When Tobias was done with his shift, he decided to visit his High School. It was early morning, so the High School front doors had just opened. Therefore, he stood outside his vehicle bent over, while wiping his front car tag. Finally, the M.A.C insignia was able to be read again on his front vehicle. Then, students began arriving for school. For every fourth or fifth student who entered the High School, there was some student who recognized him. Tobias heard a loud greeting, "Hello, Booty Guard or Good morning, Booty Guard". It made Tobias feel good. So, Tobias replied to the students, "Good morning, students!" Then, he observed some students wearing Tee Shirts with the Booty Guard words engraved on the back side. Tobias smiled and repeated, "Thank you, God because the Booty Guards were present. No sex victims will occur here".

The End (Phase 1)

FINAL REMARKS

Appreciation Request

Deborah Jackson – Mother

Richard Jackson – Father

Pricenrena Jackson – Deceased Spouse

Chontaye Jackson – Daughter

Tequila Jackson - Daughter

Bobby Jackson – Brother

Rosalind Jackson -Sister In-Law

Rodney Lawson – Brother In-Law

Lisa Lawson – Sister In-Law

Special thanks to my Aunts – Arnethia Coplin/Audrey Wilkins

City of Winston – Salem, NC

Thanks to God for the glory.